FOUND BY THE SURLY RANGER

HALEY TRAVIS

1

KARA

What a way to go. I might honestly freeze to death because this paper map is useless.

How the heck did our ancestors use the sky to find north when it's completely cloudy? I really should've paid more attention to that summer camp orienteering talk when I was nine.

Another blast of wind attacks my tiny one-person tent. I tried to find a rocky outcrop to block the breeze, but nature apparently didn't read the same survival guide I skimmed before coming here.

It's getting dark fast. Even with my flashlight, this is probably my last good chance to pee. Pulling my beanie on tightly, I abandon my tent to go out into the forest.

The fragrance has been all around me since I arrived, but it hits me all over again, fresh, damp, and lush. Until yesterday, I didn't realize that the color green really does have its own scent, and I think I'm in love with it. After the stress I've been through, it's almost relaxing.

About fifty feet from the tent, I dig a small trench with my heel, pee carefully, then kick leaves and dirt over that spot when I'm finished. I click my flashlight on again and start walking back toward my tent.

Suddenly in the gentle rustle of the deep woods, I hear a twig snap. I freeze. Then I hear another.

Don't worry. It's not him. It can't be.

I try to calm my breathing, but my heart has jumped up into my throat. There's no way he could find me here. But then, he's clever, and a self-proclaimed expert at everything.

Walking as quietly as I can, I approach my tent from the rear. It looks like the wind is really shaking it.

Then I stifle a gasp as a giant beast of a man pulls his head out of the front flap and stands up to look at me. His eyes lock with mine in the fading light. "Don't run." The command is startling. "I won't hurt you, but you'll hurt yourself running in the dark."

There is no way I could disobey that gruff tone. My feet are so rooted to the ground they might as well be in two blocks of ice.

He approaches slowly, always keeping his hands in view. There's just enough light for me to get a decent look at his huge shoulders, rugged jawline, and piercing eyes. He's absolutely *striking*—

He's also twice my size, and I'm alone in the dark with him.

"This isn't a campground, you know." His dark growl says that he means business, but his whole demeanor softens slightly as soon as he gets a better look at me. At five foot nothing, it's obvious I'm not a threat.

"I'm sorry." I shift from foot to foot. "It was kind of an emergency."

His eyes narrow as he peers around. "What kind of emergency?" I don't answer. "At least tell me, are you injured?"

"No. I'm fine."

He comes another few steps closer, and his stern expression eases a bit. "Pretty sure you're not a poacher..." It almost seems like he's trying to force a smile to put me at ease. "Few years ago there were a bunch prowling around up here. But you don't look big enough to lift a bobcat or a deer."

"No. I... Please don't turn me in. I need..." Swallowing hard, I can't even finish the thought.

"Don't worry, I won't. But there's a frost warning tonight. You can't stay here. I'll help you get back to your car."

"I can't..." I don't know what it is about this giant man, but he seems solid and for some reason trustworthy. "I had to abandon my car."

"Well..." His thick brows knit together. "There's a tiny hotel in Old Hemlock Valley. I can take you there?"

"They'll ask for my name, and I...I just can't..."

He nods slowly. "You're on the run." His huge hand runs through his dark hair as he looks down at his work boots for a moment. "Seriously, you could freeze to death if you stayed out here tonight."

My hands are clenching and unclenching, and I can't meet his eyes. "I need to stay hidden."

He exhales loudly and holds out a huge hand to shake mine. It's warm and firm, and for a split second I feel a glimmer of hope that he might help me. Then he blinks, looks down, and smells his palm. "Hand sanitizer?"

"Y-yeah."

He nods. "Got it." There's a grinding sound in his throat that might be his attempt at a half chuckle. "I'm Jace. Jace Wolfe."

My mouth opens and closes again. I have to tell him something. "Kara."

"Okay, Kara-with-no-last-name. You're on the run, but

I'm assuming you'd still rather not die tonight. Where can I take you?"

"Nowhere with Wi-Fi or cameras."

His stern eyes soften. "So it's like that." He reaches out to give me a gentle pat on the side of my shoulder. "It's okay. I've got you."

"What does that mean?"

"It means I know somewhere safe where you can stay. I'll explain on the way. We need to get going before it's completely dark. You're already shivering."

There's no denying that I need help. And somehow he feels trustworthy. Which is a comforting if unexpected feeling, given that I've been dealing with such a deceitful person over the past few months.

Jace is so focused on his self-appointed mission to care for a girl he just met in the woods that it makes me relax a bit, even as I consider that I'm following a giant stranger into a darkening forest. It doesn't hurt that the more I see of his face, the more I realize he's beyond gorgeous. He's *stunning*.

"Okay. Thank you."

2

JACE

Kara is clearly in some sort of trouble, probably being stalked. It's none of my business, yet I'm beyond curious. However, answers are going to have to wait until I get her warm and safe.

We quickly pack up her things, as I try with little success not to stare at her too much. Even in the last few minutes of what passes for daylight deep in the forest on a cloudy day, I can tell that she's beautiful, and she moves gracefully as she tosses everything into a massive backpack.

I have the tent disassembled and down in seconds, stuffing it in its bag and shouldering it with the rest of her things. Then I take her duffel bag. It's heavier than I expected. "What's in this, pretty rocks that you picked up along the way?"

"Oh. Um. A couple of books?"

I realize I'm almost chuckling. I'd never be this way with any other hiker that I found off the trail. There's something about Kara that just makes me feel... I'm not even sure what to call it yet. But there's a lot of it.

As we hurry along the path, she asks, "What about you?

Why were you out here? Were you really on the lookout for poachers?"

I can't stifle my snort. "There's a lot of people out here on Maple Trail. Some of them know what they're doing. Others don't. So a bunch of us take turns checking the trail before dark, to make sure nobody's gotten lost, or is lying there with a sprained ankle. I live the closest, so I'm here the most."

"Oh! So you're a forest ranger?"

My head tilts to look down at her, smiling up at me so brightly. "Unofficially, yeah, more or less."

We get to the trailhead, and I stash her things in the back of my pickup, then open the passenger side door for her. There's a street light in the parking lot, and as I stand in front of Kara, and finally get a better look at her, my breath stops.

It's like a halo of light encircling an angel. She's positively breathtaking.

Her long dark hair frames a beautiful, delicate face that seems to reflect the light. Her dreamy eyes are a lovely clear blue, lighter in the center, becoming darker around the edges. They're hypnotic.

Usually my energy is focused on avoiding outsiders as politely as I can. It's odd, but I want to wrap this girl in my arms, pull her against me, and discover precisely where and how her head would fit against my chest. Exhaling sharply to clear my mind, I help her up into the truck, getting a perfect view of...oh wow...her voluptuous ass.

Walking around to the driver's side is hugely uncomfortable. I haven't had a sudden erection like this just from glancing at a woman in years.

On the drive to my house, I realize just how protective of

her I already feel. What the hell happened to her to make her hide in the woods, in the cold?

"So," she says softly, "your last name is Wolfe. I've seen that name on all sorts of signs around here. Like, for businesses. You have a big family?"

"Yeah." I'm not sure how much to tell her. I don't want to sound like I'm bragging, but I also want her to feel safe. Glancing over, I notice her hands are twisting and turning over themselves.

"My family owns a huge chunk of this mountain," I explain. "Generations of passing down land, establishing various businesses. It's the kind of family that everybody knows, and nobody would mess with, you know? Which means you are totally safe on my property."

She looks over at me anxiously. "Really?"

"Really." I reach out and make a point of untangling her hands and placing them flat on her knees. She lets out a soft laugh.

"Plus, if anyone's chasing you, well, we don't know each other, so why would you come to me for help? Right?"

Kara brightens, nodding. "That makes sense. Thank you."

We get to my house just as a cold drizzle starts. Kara doesn't wait for me to help her down, leaping out of the truck and dashing to the front porch. I grab her bags, let us in, and turn on the lights before we both kick off our shoes.

Once she looks around, she visibly relaxes. My house is simple – lots of wood, sturdy, plain furniture that is still very comfortable, and huge windows overlooking the valley. "See? Just a normal house, nothing creepy," I snort.

She nods sheepishly. "Sorry."

"No sorry. I'm a total stranger. Hey – you can use my laptop if you want to Google me or something?"

Her eyes fly wide open. "You have Wi-Fi here?"

Right. She doesn't like that. Striding to the corner of the dining room where I keep my laptop, I yank all of the cables out of the modem. "Not anymore, I don't." I pull out my phone and put it in airplane mode, then hold it out to her. "See? Course, that means you can't Google me now."

She smiles a weak smile and sinks into an easy chair. "Thank you. I'm sorry. I don't mean to be difficult."

"You're obviously going through a rough patch. Let me help you. Did you have a decent dinner?"

Her head shakes sadly. "I might have been living on granola bars for the past several days."

The thought of this sweet girl going hungry makes me want to... I don't know. Growl. Punch something. She needs to be nurtured.

"Is there anything you don't eat?"

"No. But you don't have to feed me, I—"

"Listen." She blinks in surprise at the authoritative note in my voice. I place my hands up high on my hips, and tower over her so dramatically that she laughs. "There are rules in this house, missy. You will eat as much as you want and drink as much as you want. You will be comfortable. You will help yourself to everything. I demand that you be relaxed and cozy."

Kara's sudden little laugh fills me with pride. Caring for her already feels incredible – a bright spot of heat centered in my chest. I've never been a people person. I mostly keep to myself. People in town know me as a loner who takes care of his section of the forest, and is just polite enough to get by. Yet suddenly I feel myself needing to connect with Kara. More importantly, make her laugh like that with me again so that she feels safe.

"Okay. Thank you."

Snapping my fingers in her face rudely, I point to the hallway. "So here's the deal. *I'm* going to make dinner. *You're* going to take a hot bath after being out in the cold for so long." She laughs again, then pulls a face as if she's mad at the idea.

I set her up with fresh towels, and an armful of t-shirts, sweatshirts, shorts and sweatpants she can choose from.

As I lay everything on the bathroom counter, Kara gazes up at me with huge, tender eyes. "Thank you," she whispers softly. "This is the first in a long time where I feel like I can take a breath."

Damn, she's beautiful. I know she doesn't need my own powerful feelings on top of everything else she's got going on, but this attraction is bigger than anything I've had to deal with before. Reaching out, my palm cups her cheek as my thumb strokes her petal-soft skin for just a split second before I snatch my hand away again. "You're safe here. I promise." Her smile makes my heart practically explode out of my chest as I head for the kitchen to give her some space.

Cooking dinner for my mystery girl Kara underscores several facts I've been avoiding for quite some time.

I love being alone, yet I've started to become lonely. Hearing someone splashing in the bathtub actually fills me with joy. Plus, she's truly beautiful, and it's not just her physical appearance. There's something about Kara's energy... this unusual feeling that we just "click"...all of that mystical junk that I usually tune out whenever anyone brings it up.

I feel like she's mine. Like the reason I was put on this Earth was to give her a safe haven...and make her spinach salad, plus beef rotini with tomato and pepper sauce.

Kara comes out of the bathroom just as I'm setting our dinner on the table. My mouth falls open as I stare at her, then I clamp it shut fast. Her damp hair is piled up on her head in a clip, and although she's drowning in my clothing, she's rolled up the sleeves in a jaunty way, and cinched the track pants somehow so that they stay in place.

It's hot as fuck to see her in my clothes. That feeling of possession overtakes me again – a deep, primal need I've never experienced before. I'll have to shove these feelings down for now. Possibly forever, depending on her situation.

"High fashion it ain't," she says with a grin. "But it's definitely warm and cozy. Thank you."

"You're very welcome. Now, phase two of operation comfort zone treatment – dig in."

I definitely get the sense that Kara doesn't want to talk about what she's running from, so I start the conversation off with some thoughts about recent movies. Once we get chatting, I discover that she's a voracious reader. Luckily, we've both read some of the latest bestselling mysteries, so we dissect who we thought the murderer was at various points, and why. She laughs uproariously at how neither one of us saw *the twist* coming. Then, suddenly, her eyes drop.

Whatever has upset her, I instantly want to tear it apart with my bare hands. "What is it?"

Her luscious bottom lip quivers. "It's just... Sometimes life really throws you a twist of your own, doesn't it?"

"That it does." My hand covers hers until she looks at me. "Whatever is going on, we're going to figure it out."

"Oh, it's not your problem to figure out," she sputters. "I don't want to get you involved with—"

My hand squeezes hers gently. "I am the ruler of this house and part of this mountain, and I decree that we are going to figure it out."

Damn, I love the way this beautiful woman laughs.

"Now, I'm afraid my guestroom is a disaster area that

would take hours to sort out. So you're taking my bed, and I'll sleep on the—"

She holds her hand up in front of my face like a traffic cop. "Listen, mister ruler of the house and part of the mountain. You're being incredibly sweet, and I super appreciate it. Now, I'm no engineer, but considering your height, my height, and the size of your couch, I am much better off there. End of discussion."

My mouth opens to protest, and she snaps her fingers in my face just as rudely as I did to her before while giggling. I laugh so hard I surprise myself. Why does being snappy and rude to each other like this feel so terrific? It's that click again. The connection. The way it feels like I've already known her for a very long time.

"Bossy little thing," I growl, standing up. "I'll get her royal highness some blankets." By the time I bring back the softest sheets and a fluffy comforter, Kara has already cleared the dishes and loaded the dishwasher. "You didn't have to do that."

She gives me a positively withering look with her hand on one hip as she gestures broadly at the entire house. "And you didn't have to do this. So there."

I make up the couch for her, and watch curiously as she digs out one of her books and sets it on the coffee table before sliding in between the covers. "In case I can't sleep," she explains.

"Good point. Help yourself to anything you need, and feel free to wake me up if you can't find anything." I click on the small lamp on the end table and switch off the overhead lights. "Warm enough?"

"Toasty as fresh toast." Her wide smile releases a flood of raw emotion I didn't know I was capable of. I would do anything to scoop her into my arms and take her to my own bed right now. Not just to get her naked, although I can't stop thinking about that, but just to be near her. To hold her. To make sure that nothing would ever make her feel unsafe again. That's definitely going to take more than a few hours and one dinner.

"Thank you for everything, Jace," she says softly, her eyes luminous in the dim light. "You've taken me on one of my worst days ever and brought me to a wonderfully cozy oasis. I appreciate it."

My heart swells with warmth again. "You're very welcome. Good night."

Once I'm settled in bed, I can't help thinking about how much better it would be if she was here forever. How much better my life would be if I could keep her here permanently.

Plenty of people have told me that I need a woman in my life, and I've always shrugged them off. I've never needed a woman.

But apparently I've always needed Kara.

3

KARA

Holy crap. I haven't slept so well in weeks. Maybe ever.

The rain slowly lulled me to sleep with a calm tapping on the roof. I did wake up wide-eyed and shaking in the middle of the night, the stress of the past week flooding back. But once I heard Jace snoring from the other room, it only took a few minutes for me to settle down, and I'd fallen back asleep before I knew it.

The light filtering through the trees outside definitely signals that it's morning. I jump up, brush my hair, and put on coffee as silently as possible. It feels weird not to have a phone to check the time. Or the weather. It makes me feel...untethered.

Jace, on the other hand, makes me feel completely grounded. What would it feel like to have an anchor like that around all the time?

Safe. Definitely safe. Even though he's clearly a gruff, loner type. I'm picking up that he's trying to be friendly with me, though. That's sweet, to make the effort.

If I told any of my friends that I'd slept at a stranger's

house they would think I'm nuts. And yet, although I don't claim to be able to read people or anything, Jace's eyes are so...open. He's clearly a no nonsense, straight shooter – except when he's joking around with me, which is ridiculous and endearing.

I'm just putting the finishing touches on the scrambled eggs as Jace walks stiffly out of the bedroom, running a hand absently through his thick, dark hair.

In the morning light, his eyes are a deep forest green. My eyes accidentally drop to the front of his navy pajama pants, and...oh boy... I'm going to have to pretend that massive moving shadow is a trick of the light. Otherwise, I might never be able to concentrate again.

"Hey." His voice is even deeper, still rough from sleep. "You made coffee. I didn't just dream you." He fills a mug, somehow managing to get completely in my way in the enormous kitchen as he pulls milk from the fridge. "What are you making?"

"Secret special breakfast surprise." I back into him to shove him aside. The warmth of his chest against the back of my shoulder is enough to make me quiver. How can he be this sexy?

"This morning is when you're going to spill all your secrets, so you might as well start by telling me what we're having for breakfast." He frowns as he watches my expression fall. "Sorry. Bad joke. Didn't mean to upset you."

My head shakes as I shove him gently toward the table. "I know you didn't. Just let me get another mug of coffee in me, then I'll tell you everything." I set a plate in front of him. "Secret breakfast surprise. I'll give you a hint: you're officially out of English muffins. They're the best for scrambled egg sandwiches."

"Thanks. This looks amazing."

We eat in silence for a few minutes, watching the sun slowly drag itself up over the trees to the east. I realize I might as well spit it out.

"I'm on the run because I was going into business with someone I thought was a friend. Well, more like a friend of a friend. Brad Brown. But everything went sideways."

Jace sips his coffee, nodding. "What kind of business was it?"

Staring into my coffee mug, my entire body sags. I feel so stupid about this whole mess.

"It's okay." His rough voice is gentler now. "Take your time."

"I thought it was such a good idea. It's almost like a dating app but for art." Jace stares at me, puzzled, waiting for me to continue.

"Many people don't know anything about art, but they want something in their homes. So it was designed for them to use any kind of descriptors. Large format, vertical, abstract, nature, realism. Stuff like that. Some people would love a colorful piece to make the dining room look put together, but they don't know how to explain what they want."

I smile to myself. "I've always loved all kinds of art, and it seemed like such a great idea. With this app users could tap a vague prompt, like light blue, or seaside, even "weird", and it'll display a selection of pieces for them to choose from. High resolution prints of original works. They pay for the rights, then they can have it printed and framed locally." My fingernails are tapping against the edge of the mug, and I force myself to stop. "Galleries, printers and framers were already lining up for ad space."

"Sounds terrific. What went wrong?"

"I found out Brad was already planning to send people

directly to galleries and printers in his network that are owned by his cousins and stuff. Which wasn't the point of the app at all – it was supposed to lift all artists, and help all kinds of printers."

I'm sure Jace can tell how upset I feel from the look on my face. "Plus, I may have inadvertently overheard a phone call that he was planning on cutting me out of it as soon as it took off."

"So... The short version is, Brad is a total jackass?"

"Yep," I sigh. "My friends all said that he was this tech genius dude. And the thing is, he *is*. The guy can figure anything out. But it turns out he's also kind of psychotic. Or...as someone else called it...a narcissistic sociopath."

"Either way, definitely not someone you should be involved with," Jace says softly.

"Exactly. He was wheeling and dealing with his family, and he wanted to take my idea, toss me out, and make a ton of money."

"When it was all your idea and you did all of the work."

"Right?! Months of research, sourcing artists that weren't in galleries, getting the ball rolling with advertisers and starting the process of getting listed in the Apple and Google app stores. So much prep work. I mean, yeah, he did the programming and coded the search functions...but he also did some weird back door thing that would track people's purchases on other websites so that he could pass that information along to third parties to make even more cash."

Jace's eyes widen, his jaw tightening. "So he intended to spy on his customers?"

"Yeah. Which means he was also probably spying on me."

"Which is why you took off."

"Yeah." I take a sip of coffee before admitting, "I *may* have hacked into his email. If you can call it hacking when he left his laptop unattended to take a call outside."

Jace snorts. "That's not hacking. That's fair game."

"Anyway, I used the opportunity to remove his access to the database and changed all of the passwords, making them so long and complicated it would take months to crack even with one of those code busting things."

"And now you're terrified that he's after you?"

"Well...yes." I shrug, looking at him despondently. "His connections are going to be after him if he doesn't deliver on his promises, right? I figured if I completely disappeared, he might give up in a few weeks. I drove to the base of Wolfe Mountain because I don't know anybody here. I printed a paper map that turned out to be less than helpful and left my phone and laptop in the car, even though I've wiped them. Everything he's after is now only stored in the cloud."

Jace looks at me carefully, then reaches out to take my hand. "Tell me, Kara. If this guy really is a psycho, how far do you think he will go to find you?"

"I don't know," I sputter. "Sometimes he's fixated on one thing for a really long time. Other times he drops an idea after two days and jumps to another one. He's all over the place. But this time he has a bunch of other people to answer to."

His hand squeezes mine again, then he pulls back, staring up at the ceiling for a moment, thinking. "If I were to use cell service for just a minute, could you get me a photo of this guy?"

"Sure. It's all over his website."

"Even better. What's the site?"

"BradBrownTechnology.com."

He reaches over to where he left his phone charging last

night. "I'm going to text a handful of people. Then it's going right back into airplane mode. Okay?"

I find it deeply touching that he clearly knows what's best, yet still asks for my permission. "Sure. Thank you."

He calls up the website and finds a photo of Brad. "That him?"

I flinch. "Yeah."

He uses voice to text to send a similar message to three different people. "Hey – go to bradbrowntechnology.com and take a good look at the photos of the guy. If you see him around, don't let on that anything's up, just tell me where he is."

His thumb flips back to the photo of Brad in his expensive suit, wearing a shit-eating office-appropriate grin. A shudder runs down my spine when I remember the way he screamed at me.

Jace smirks and scoffs. "Yeah, you're definitely safe with me, beautiful. I could take him out with one shot." He twitches slightly, as if he didn't mean to put it that way. Then his phone rings. "It's my younger brother." He presses the button and turns up the volume so I can hear. "Hey, Josh."

"Jace, what's with this Brad guy? Are you in some kind of trouble?"

"Not me. There's a chance he's after a woman who has information he wants. He's a scumbag, so I'm keeping an eye on her."

"Do you need help, or just a lookout?"

"Just a lookout for now."

"Got it. I'll spread the word."

"Thanks. And can you ask the others to check the trails for me? Oh, and my phone's gonna be in airplane mode most of the time, so I might be slow getting back to you."

"Got it. Oh shit – if you've been offline, then you probably haven't heard about the bridge being out from all of the rain last week, then again last night. I'll holler when it's clear."

"Thanks. Talk soon."

He disconnects, then notices my fingers are twitching. "The bridge is out?"

"It's fine," he murmurs, reaching out to cup my cheek again. Every time he touches my skin I feel sparks flying through every part of me. Certain parts more than others. I've never been so close to such a sexy man, and it's making me feel...I dunno. Like my body is starved for touch and aching for more.

"There's two roads into town: a super winding back one that's pretty dangerous, and a much safer direct one. But it has a bridge over a river that rises fast when we get more than two days of rain and sometimes washes out. Don't worry – I have supplies here for six weeks or more. It'll probably only be out for a day or three." He pulls his hand away, just as I realize I'm pressing my cheek into it. "I mean, you're hiding out anyway, right?"

"Fair." I nod. "Maybe it's a good thing."

"There you go."

My stomach lurches as I realize I'll be stuck here with Jace for a few days. He won't be off checking the trails or going into town to run errands. We'll be alone, without much else to do. My mind is already racing at the implications.

Proximity breeds familiarity.

And I already know that I want Jace to be just as familiar with me as he wants.

4

JACE

Every few years there are noises about updating the old bridge, usually right after it washes out, but it's typically only a twenty-four hour inconvenience at most.

This time, it can stay out for weeks, for all I care. My only project for the next little while is to convince Kara that I'm the man for her. That she should stay here with me forever. Even though I realize it's not logical to have those kinds of thoughts so fast.

We load the dishwasher and hand wash a few things that won't fit, then Kara puts on another pot of coffee. We already work well together, which makes me feel like we have great potential. But if she's already dealing with one borderline psycho who is trying to steal her intellectual property, I need to be extremely careful that she doesn't feel trapped with me.

I can't make any sort of move until I get a clear sign. Which means she'll basically need to wave a green flag right in my face. I don't know much about women, and haven't dated in years. Crap, I hope I'll recognize today's version of a green flag.

It occurs to me that my habit of pretty much avoiding people over the past several years has further damaged my already limited small talk skills. Time to push down my usual stoic, silent demeanor and force myself to be chattier.

"So, shall I check my phone again to confirm that my guys are on the lookout?"

Kara instantly looks uncomfortable. "Um. That would be two pings from your phone in the same place, though."

"Right. Okay, what do you think about going for a drive? Or maybe a walk?"

Kara brightens. "Oh! I'd love to go for a walk in the forest with somebody who actually knows the area so I know we won't get lost."

My traitorous right hand involuntarily stretches out to stroke the back of her hand where it rests on the counter. "I hate that you were lost in the forest, Kara. Out there alone and cold, not even with a phone."

Is it just wishful thinking, or do her eyes light up when she looks at me? "I'm so lucky that you found me."

"I'm lucky too." Damn, the urge to grab her and yank her against me makes me feel like a barely in control caveman. Her perfect lips are so close to me, teasing me, demanding that I make a move—

"Bundle up, it's going to be chilly after the rain."

Once we get walking, it gets a lot easier to chat lightly with Kara. She tells me about her two years at university, accidentally mentioning in the process that she's twenty-two years old. She tells me about her tiny apartment in the city where the only window opens onto the brick wall of the building next door. Obviously, that doesn't thrill me. This sweet darling girl needs proper access to fresh outdoor air.

"It's so magical out here!" she exclaims as we reach the crest of a hill about a mile from my house.

Looking around, the rugged terrain of the side of the mountain has always filled me with a deep sense of peace and belonging. Probably because this is what I've seen from every window since I was born.

Kara's arms stretch out as she twirls slowly in a circle. "This place makes me want to start singing. It's ridiculous. It's like I'm high from all the fresh air."

She's such a bright spark. For half a second, I wonder with a pang if I'm not actually the right man for her – if my relatively boring life and routines would drag her down and dim her light. Then I push the disastrous thought away.

Taking my phone out of airplane mode, I quickly flip through a handful of texts. "Nobody has seen Brad yet," I confirm. "Oh, good – Josh has given the photo to Griffin at the gas station. Most people who come through stop for gas at some point. Do you know what kind of car he drives?"

"A Silver Mercedes."

I text that info to my brother, and directly to Griffin. Then I glance at Kara with a snort. "Yeah, good luck driving *that* thing around the mountain roads. I doubt it could handle the potholes when—"

"Look!" Kara points a trembling finger to a speck in the sky as the familiar buzzing rattle and chop of a helicopter coming closer.

I'm about to explain when I notice that Kara's eyes have filled with tears, her hands clenched into shaky fists. I flick my phone back into airplane mode, drop it into my pocket, then slip an arm around her. "Let's go."

I hurry her into the forest, under the cover of trees. Then I find one of the larger, rocky outcrops that forms a ledge that we can duck under. It's just tall enough for me to stand up straight.

Kara is still shaking. "Come here." My arms open wide and she darts into them, twisting so that she's between my body and the rock.

"It's okay. I know that helicopter. I see it every three to five weeks. They do mountain photography when it's clear out, especially the day after it rains because everything looks extra lush and green. I only brought you over here because I saw you were panicking."

Kara looks up at me, her bottom lip wobbling. "Are you sure?"

"Pretty darn positive. That chopper looked blue. News helicopters are usually black or white. All the rescue choppers around here are red and white. And I can't think of any reason why a private plane would be up here."

"Unless..." Her bottom lip is trembling, and my thumb automatically goes to stroke it gently.

"Would Brad really spend the money on a helicopter to go after you?" I can feel her shoulders heaving as she tries to hold back her sobs.

"I didn't tell you everything," she whispers. "Some of the art galleries Brad was setting up deals with... They're involved with money laundering. One of his cousins has gotten in with the mafia, and they were all excited about a new method of cleaning their money. Apparently it's one of the easiest ways to do it."

Well, shit. Holding her tightly against me, I stroke her back gently. The chopper gets louder, then the noise fades away to nothing. "Hear that? A search plane would go in circles. They went straight across."

Kara dabs at her eyes with her sleeve, then looks up at

me sheepishly. "I'm sorry. You must think I'm completely paranoid."

I tip up her chin with my finger. "Not at all. I swore that I would keep you safe, and part of that includes making you feel comfortable any time something startles you. Okay?" The soft smile that blooms across her lips almost makes me feel dizzy. Damn, she's so beautiful it's hard to think straight.

"You ducked under the trees even though you knew the helicopter had nothing to do with me? You're a really decent guy, Jace."

My head shakes automatically. "Ask anyone in town, beautiful. I'm a grumpy loner who grumbles every time I find clueless idiots on the trails, and doesn't keep in touch with his family enough."

"Well, you're a really decent guy to me."

My head is already dipping lower. "Does a decent guy steal a kiss from a gorgeous girl who is terrified and rattled?"

My heart stops until she nods. "I think so. Distraction technique, right?"

I don't even care if she's teasing. Her gorgeously curvaceous body fits against me perfectly as I hold her closer, her firm round breasts pressed against my chest. Our lips meet softly, and she lets out a tiny sigh. As we melt together, the kiss takes on a life of its own.

The taste of her lush lips fills me with raw, unbridled lust. It tears through me, sending sharp images into my mind. Images of Kara's legs spread as I lick her softest skin, watching her fall apart. Of her eyes wide as she comes for me. Of her soft body covered by my large frame as I take her slowly and gently.

I feel transported. Squeezing her close, our kiss deepens even more, her mouth opening for mine as I explore her softness. Every little gasp, every slight moan, makes my entire body feel harder. Stronger. I'm determined to use this newfound strength to protect this lovely girl in any way I can.

And somehow, I'm going to convince her that here with me on my mountain is the safest place for her.

Permanently.

5

KARA

I've only been kissed a handful of times, and never like this. It's like the difference between glancing at a hasty doodle on a crinkled scrap of paper, and walking into a gallery and being completely overcome by a twenty-foot painting created by a master.

Jace kisses like a *master*.

His mouth molds to mine as he searches, explores, devours. His huge, rough hands clutch at me firmly, one of them running down around my hip, then wandering across my ass. From the way his fingers dig into me, I'm pretty sure he likes my curves, thank goodness.

The kiss grows wilder, leaving me boneless and breathless as I feel his hunger, mixed with a feral, possessive energy that feels completely right. There's a faint growl in the back of his throat, as if just kissing isn't enough for him. Or is he as overwhelmed by this moment as I am?

"So hot..." he murmurs against my lips.

Really? I've never once in my life thought of myself as hot. Yet as my fingers spear through his thick hair, and my body squirms between the rock wall and the wall of muscle in front of me, that's exactly how I feel. Hot. Sexy. And *very* curious about what will happen next.

Jace grips the back of my hair, tilting my head back so he can trail kisses down the side of my throat. Then he growls again and straightens up. "A nasty part of me wants to tell you that I hear another helicopter, so that you'll stay hidden in here with me all day." He flashes me a wink. "But we're actually going to need dinner at some point." His hand slides gently down my spine. "I won't let you get cold or hungry ever again."

He takes my hand and leads me back to the trail as my mind reels. *Ever?* As in... He's hoping that I might stick around?

Back in Kingsville, the harsh reality is I don't have much of a life. A couple of friends, of course. A tiny apartment. I did a lot of research at art galleries, but that's not something I need to do every month. Most of my work was always done from the couch on my laptop.

"Hey." Jace gives my hand a bit of a shake. "You okay? You seem a million miles away, and you're missing one heck of a view."

My head swivels to the left as we stop walking. Through a handful of older trees, the view of the valley and the rolling green hills is indeed breathtaking. The rocky spikes of the mountaintop seem so close that I can almost imagine I see the texture of the stone.

"Sorry. I just realized how lost I am without my job. Phone. Laptop. Anything."

His thick arm wraps around me as I'm snuggled against his chest again. "As soon as the bridge reopens, we can take my laptop to the library and use the Wi-Fi there to email people and let them know you're okay. How does that sound?"

"Oh. Um. Maybe. Thank you."

We continue walking back, and I realize that Jace isn't afraid of *anything*. Even when I mentioned that Brad has mafia connections, he didn't flinch. The man just has no stress at all. No worries about outside forces. The only time he's looked worried is when he figured I was cold and hungry.

I squeeze his strong hand. "Hey... Can I make you a fancy dinner tonight?"

Walking across the wild patch of meadow that serves as his backyard, he smiles down at me. "But you're my guest. Aren't I supposed to cook for you?"

"I've been too busy to cook for months. Plus, you have that massive kitchen."

"Not so massive."

"Please." I roll my eyes as we step inside and kick off our shoes. "Your kitchen is practically the size of my entire apartment."

He scowls. "You're a tiny girl, but that doesn't sound big enough to me."

I shrug. "I didn't make a lot as a waitress before I went to Brad with my idea. The weekly salary he gave me so I could focus on this project was based more on what I had been making as a waitress than what the work was actually worth, I think."

Looking down, I'm surprised at the look in Jace's eyes as he stares angrily at the floor. "If I ever find that guy, I'm going to have some very loud and not-very-polite words for him." His face softens as his gaze lifts to meet mine. "But I will never be angry around you, beautiful. You don't ever have to worry about that."

I swear, every time I smile, his eyes light up. "We're always supposed to trust the forest ranger, right?"

He chuckles and shakes his head as we walk into the kitchen. "That's right. You think I'm a ranger."

"Hey, you said yourself that you patrol the trails all the time. That you're looking out for people, and looking out for the forest. That makes you a ranger in my books."

"Does it count if it's only a volunteer position?"

I lift my chin, nodding seriously. "I say yes. And as the temporary queen of this kitchen, you're about to tell me what food I have access to. Then I'm kicking you out."

I expect Jace to smirk as usual. Instead, he drops to one knee, taking my hand and kissing the back of it reverently. "Of course, my queen."

My hands and heart flutter as he gets back up, showing me where everything is and what meat is already defrosted. "There you go. I'll go to try and clear up the guest room in the meantime."

I can't help but be curious: I want to know everything there is to know about this breathtaking, sexy man. "Wait. May I see what this famous mess is?"

He shrugs. "Sure."

He takes me to the guest room and opens the door, and I blink in surprise. I was expecting boxes of knickknacks, or piles of out of season clothing. Instead, the bed, desk, and part of the floor are all covered with paperwork in tidy stacks. Notes. Maps. And... "Are those pictures of birds?"

He slouches against the door frame, nodding wryly. "Yeah. My friend Barrett and his new... *special friend*...have an idea to fix the Old Hemlock Valley tourism issue. So I've gone into full on research mode."

Turning to face him, I poke the center of his chest with my index finger. "See? You *are* a ranger. You adore this town, and you're protecting it. Kind of like...a police officer of the forest."

Jace tries to pull his face into a scowl, but fails dismally. His eyes are twinkling. "You're a very strange woman."

I turn to leave, and then stop. "Honestly? Don't put away your research. It was really comfortable on the couch, and I'd feel terrible about messing up your workflow."

A thick eyebrow lifts. "You want to tell me what to do in the rest of my house? It'll cost you."

Oh my god, does this man even know what he *does* to my heart rate? Oddly, it gives me a sudden rush of bravery. I step closer, slowly placing my hands in the center of his chest. Then I slide them up to his shoulders as my chin lifts, catching his lips with mine. It's a soft, delicate kiss, yet it sends tingles all the way through me.

Pulling away, he smiles. "If that's how you pay a man, I'm going to start charging for every sip of water and breath of air you take here."

"I'll think about it." Turning away, I toss my head and flick my hair behind me, eliciting that low, raspy chuckle that I think I'm already becoming addicted to.

Even though my focus should be on straightening out my present situation, I can't help but think about the future. Is there any chance that I could end up staying here with Jace? Any chance that he'd want an artsy, curvy, silly nobody like me?

Any chance that, coming out of this giant mess, my life could take a turn for the better instead of the worse just for once?

6

JACE

I'd forgotten that I owned candles until Kitchen Queen summoned me for dinner and I saw the table set nicely with flickering tea lights.

I'd also been lost in my notes for so long that I didn't even notice that she changed at some point. Kara now stands in front of me in a bright peach-colored dress, her hair twisted half up in a clip, and a smudge of brown eye makeup that makes the blue of her eyes even more intense.

Reaching for her feels like the most natural thing in the world. My arms pull her close, kissing her gently as I feel her sexy body instantly pressed close against mine. "You didn't need to go to this much trouble, gorgeous. But it's very sweet of you."

Her smile warms me from the inside out. "Well, I didn't know how long it had been since you'd had someone cook for you."

"I go to Fran's...that's the diner in town...at least once a week. Plus dinner at Mom's maybe once a month." My lips sweep a slow looping path around the shell of her ear, then I nuzzle just below. "And I'm about to be investing in a friend's restaurant soon. I can't wait to take you on a proper date there. Or anywhere else you like, really. How about we go for a scenic drive to Spring Grove and I take you to the Evergreen Pub for a fantastic steak dinner someday?"

Kara smiles shyly. "I'm certainly not a dating expert, by any stretch. But maybe we could pretend tonight?"

"Baby, this isn't pretending, and you know it."

I can't believe how much trouble she went to. Fresh spinach, walnut and pear salad. Fresh-baked (!!!) herbed rolls. Lasagna. She even found the good dishes.

We sit down, and I reach out to squeeze her knee. "You are the most beautiful woman I've ever seen, Kara."

Her cheeks turn an adorable shade of pink, her eyes glowing in the candlelight. "You can't mean that."

"I do indeed. Which is why I am about to lay down the law here."

She looks at me, pursing her lips and arching her eyebrows, as if she already suspects I'm going to say something ridiculous.

"You're breathtaking. Sexy. Sweet and smart. And now you're trying to show off by being a brilliant chef as well. That's just out of line. I'm going to have to insist that you settle down."

She crosses her arms, subtly kicking my shin. "Eat your dinner before it gets cold," she commands.

Reaching out, I gently grab the shoulder of her dress, pulling her toward me for a slow, sultry kiss. "There. I was more hungry for you than for the food, delicious as it looks."

Her eyes snap closed as her cheeks redden again. "Let's eat."

Just a few bites of salad, and I'm in Heaven. Kara licks a miniscule walnut fragment from her bottom lip, and half of my blood instantly rushes south. She has no idea how irresistibly sexy she is. "So," I ask, "since the app you've been working on isn't going to pan out, what are your plans for the future now?"

"I don't know. I've always wanted to work on something in art and tech, but I'm not a programmer. I guess I'll have to go back to waitressing for now."

"Do you love it?"

"No, but I'm okay at it. It pays for my apartment, food, books." Her lips are so inviting when she smirks. "Occasional frivolous purchases like lip balm, or a new sweater."

"If you're not super attached to Kingsville, perhaps you might consider moving someday?" I'm probably being too blunt, but I need to know that it's at least a possibility.

Her perfect white teeth sink into her bottom lip for a moment. "I guess. I mean, there's nothing really tying me there."

"Good. That's all I need to know. For now."

We dig in, alternating between eating, chatting, and staring into each other's eyes. This connection between us feels magical. This is what has been missing from my life, and I wasn't even bright enough to realize it.

After dinner, I insist on taking care of cleanup while she lounges on the couch. Then I start a fire, and we fall down an amazing rabbit hole of sharing hilarious stories from our childhoods. I tell her about some of the weird and wonderful things that have happened on the mountain with my extended family. Kara tells me funny anecdotes from her University days with her friends, even though it sounds like most of them have moved away.

Then she sighs in exasperation. "That's why I thought Brad was trustworthy. He was a friend of Steven's, and he and I were such great buddies at school."

I stiffen momentarily, picturing her at school with who knows how many guys looking at her. I've never felt so possessive about anyone before. "I get it. We want to trust friends of friends. But you never know if their radar for who's good and who's not is calibrated the same way as yours."

She nods. "Exactly. I feel like an absolute idiot now for trusting him. I should have paid more attention to the way he was getting fussier and meaner. I should've looked into his other companies instead of just taking his word for it. I should have—"

Her hands are beginning to twitch, and I reach out to hold them. "Don't beat yourself up. It's okay. You're safe on my mountain now."

She sniffles slightly. "Yeah. But for how long, though?"

I spread my arms wide. "Want to hide out in here?"

"Does that make me a baby if I want to do nothing but hide?"

"No way. Think of it as a vacation from your stress. A chance to run away from it all for a few days."

She shifts into my arms, and when I sit back against the couch, she somehow ends up in my lap. I love how comfortable she is with me. It shows that she trusts me, which is not something I take lightly. "I hate seeing you so tense, baby. But I don't want to overstep any lines."

Kara shrugs. "Do I even have any lines?"

"Are you saying that I can kiss you for as long as I like?" She smiles and nods. I attempt to glower. "Okay then. You tell me when you've had enough, or if I should stop."

Her fingers walk up my t-shirt, then tickle the back of my ear as she leans in closer. "Jace, I've never felt like this with anyone before," she whispers. "Let's just go with the flow.

Not just a vacation from my stress...a vacation from the whole world. Sounds good?"

"Better than good. Sounds perfect."

As if on cue, the power flickers for a few seconds. My arms tighten around her as I kiss across her cheek. "Relax, beautiful. Sometimes it gets windy up here, and it shakes the power lines. Once in a while they go down. But don't worry – I have firewood, a backup generator, and plenty of food. You're completely safe with me, Kara."

The pressure of her delicate fingers across the back of my neck makes my breath unsteady. "I know," she whispers against my chest. "I've never felt like that with anyone. My whole life, everything has always been up in the air. And now I don't know how I'll pay my rent, and the app I worked so hard on for months is gone. And yet, with you, I feel like everything is going to be okay."

"And it will be. I promise."

My head dips down for a long, steamy kiss. My hand wanders across her hip, then slowly up to tease the bottom of her right breast over the fabric of her dress. I love that she's not wearing a bra. She moans against my lips, tilting her body as if to help me caress her.

"Am I a wicked man if I invite you to stay in my bed tonight?"

"Maybe. Am I extremely improper if I accept your invitation?"

"Maybe. But I think I like you being improper."

Reaching up, I take the clip out of her hair and set it aside as she leans back a bit and shakes out the long waves. I use the moment to my advantage, kissing along the graceful column of her throat until she is shuddering in my arms. "So sexy," I murmur. "Thank you for dinner – it was amazing. But I'm still hungry." My eyes meet hers. "I want you."

Her bottom lip wobbles for a second, then she nods decisively. "I want you too."

I'm not sure how far we're going to go tonight, but that doesn't matter. I just need sweet Kara in my arms. In my bed. In my house. In my life.

I just need her.

7

KARA

Seriously. How does Jace manage to kiss me with his *entire body*?

The way he clutches me to him feels so possessive. His rough palm caresses my lower back firmly, his warm touch flowing straight through the material. Every time I shudder, I feel a slight answering growl in his throat. He's like a wild animal, aching to let his true nature out.

Jace has talked about his friends in town, but a tiny part of me wouldn't be that surprised if I'm the first person he's spoken to, I mean *really* spoken to, in years. He just has that isolated, almost feral look in his eyes sometimes. But even with the wildness, I feel comforted somehow by the way his massive arms hold me so solidly.

His lips move slowly against mine and then our mouths open as he kisses me more deeply, his tongue gently exploring as if he's trying to bond us together. A tidal wave of lust hits me square in the center of my chest. Then lower. Much, much lower. My hips begin to squirm. Of course I've been curious about sex for ages, but I've never been presented with the opportunity to explore it with a hot guy that I trust.

Jace is everything I could've dreamed of for that, and then ten times more.

A deep shiver runs through me as I realize I'm rubbing shamelessly against the thick erection rising between us. His groan makes me smile against his lips. "You'd better not tease me right now, beautiful. It's been a long, long time."

I gasp as he scoops me up in the air, carrying me to the bedroom. The room is stark, minimalist, and full of big, heavy wood. *Kind of like Jace himself,* I think with a silent giggle. I can't stop myself from pressing against him. Knowing that I'm making him hard is lighting a fire inside my soul. Jace's hunger is a fire spreading to me as he lays me across the bed, kissing and caressing as if he never wants to stop.

Good. I don't want him to, either.

His massive, muscular frame covers me, cages me, making me feel safe and sheltered. A warm hand glides up my side, and I realize my dress has slid all the way up. The rough denim of his jeans against my bare legs feels incredible.

"Can I take this off?" His deep voice is questioning, yet it sounds like a command, not a request.

"Please do." I eagerly help him pull it off. He licks his lips wickedly when he sees I'm not wearing a bra, stretched across his bed in nothing but dark green cotton panties.

A fluttering, strained sound bubbles up from my throat as he kisses up my stomach, caressing my sensitive breasts. Then he wraps his lips around a nipple, licking and sucking just hard enough for it to feel like a slight pinch. My fingers thread through his thick hair, holding him close as he groans against my skin, almost growling.

Jace feels hungry for me, like a wild animal that hasn't been fed in years. The idea sends a thrill zipping up and down my spine, and I tremble as he switches to the other side. The way he moves so slowly, gauging every reaction I make, tells me that ultimately I'm in charge, even though he's taking control of me. His kisses become lighter, dancing up my throat to catch my lips before darting south again.

I'm so lost in what's going on that it takes me a second to realize that my panties are being pulled away from my ankles. Momentary shyness overtakes me, my knees moving to pull my thighs together as he shifts lower. Jace glowers, yet his eyes are twinkling. "I want to taste you right now. Yes?"

I'm already nodding as he parts my legs wide, getting into position. He stares at my open pussy a moment before dragging a finger slowly through the center. "So soft and sexy," he murmurs. His rough fingertips part my skin, skimming slowly along every dip and fold until I'm melting.

I adore the feeling of him taking control of my body. It's as if he already knows how I want to be touched.

His thumbs spread me open, then I stare in astonishment as Jace winks before slowly drawing his tongue straight along my crease. My fingers tighten in his hair as my hips shake, calves tightening around his broad back. I hum along with another soft growl in his throat as he begins licking me, kissing me, moving his mouth over my most delicate flesh.

I'm afraid I'll tear out his hair, so I move my hands to the blanket under me, hanging on for dear life for fear I'll float away.

"Relax, baby," he commands me, staring deeply into my eyes. He's so gorgeous. No – mesmerizing. I can't stop staring at every expression that crosses his face. "Can you come for me?"

"I'll try."

My belly flutters, nerve endings straining as warmth floods every inch of my body. Once again, he gives me that smile that I feel is deeply special and only for me. I definitely get the impression that he's a bit of a grouch with the outside world. That he doesn't let many people in. I already feel closer to him than I have with anyone else in my life. Which is wild – how bizarre to think that at one of the lowest points in my life, I would find a man who has the potential to be... I can't even think about that yet.

My spine arches as his tongue flicks gently against my clit. It feels swollen, my entire pussy open and wet.

"You're delicious," he murmurs against my skin. "Now, close your eyes and let go."

There's no way I can shut my eyes: Jace is too sexy not to look at as he's focused completely on my breathing, on the way I squirm and writhe under him. One thick arm scoops under my thigh to hold me in place. His hot, agile tongue begins to dance lightly around my clit without quite touching it, occasionally brushing straight through my pussy lips.

Every single nerve inside me tightens and twists as I stare into the eyes of the man who already seems to want to care for me and protect me forever. Then I'm falling over the cliff, thrashing as waves of bliss tumble through me. My weak cries make him lick flat against my clit while he holds me down, draining every single drop of pleasure from me.

Finally he pulls back, wiping his mouth dramatically with the back of his hand. "Now that's what I call a perfect bedtime snack."

We laugh together, then he stands up and rolls his

shoulders. "Just so you know, I never sleep in anything but my shorts. You can wear what you like, or stay naked, as long as you sleep curled up in my arms tonight. Yes?"

"Yes."

I use the bathroom, then slip one of his t-shirts over my head for a baggy nightgown. I would have expected him to want more, yet Jace seems to have decided that that's all we're doing tonight.

He kisses me softly as I snuggle into his bed, then arranges the blankets around me. "Sweet dreams, my sweet girl."

As I drift off, I wonder if he's just being charming, or if there's actually a small chance I could be "his girl". I've learned the hard way that I should never get my hopes up. That things always happen to ruin the best laid plans.

But a girl can hope, can't she?

8

JACE

I'm in a trance as I move on autopilot through the kitchen, making coffee, slicing thick oat bread for toast. As the early morning light streams in across the counter, the house is nearly silent, yet I can sense Kara's presence in the bedroom.

I can't believe this goddess appeared in my life. Can't believe I'm falling for her so hard. The connection between us is frighteningly immediate. Like a light switch being turned on.

Not to mention, it genuinely feels like she's giving me a purpose in life. I've always thought of myself as an accidental...well, not a playboy, but I'm in an extremely privileged position where I don't need to work a traditional job.

My "work", such as it is, involves maintaining my section of the forest and my house, garage, and shed. Patrolling the trails. Helping neighbors whenever they need it, of course, because that's just what you do. And staying involved with the Old Hemlock Valley Council to make sure that things keep running smoothly.

But my main focus is and always has been the forest.

Which means I really am a forest ranger. How strange that having Kara bestow this unofficial title on me makes me feel more grounded. My purpose was always there, I just needed someone to hang a sign on it for me.

As the coffee brews, I turn my phone on for just a few seconds and do a search.

Forest Ranger, n.: A person whose job involves protecting the forested area. Someone who enforces laws and rules relating to camping, hunting, and fishing. Someone who clears dead trees, replants new growth, and preserves the natural environment.

I blow out a breath. Yep. That's me.

I flick the phone back into airplane mode and drop it in the charger. Even as a kid, I was always the one who grabbed an ax to clear dead branches. Who nurtured the saplings. Who marked the trails in treacherous areas every spring.

My head jerks up as Kara slides into a seat at the kitchen island. I pour her a cup of coffee, my heart already racing from seeing her beautiful smile. "Sorry to interrupt," she murmurs softly. "You look like you were miles away."

Returning her smile, I realize I've been in the best mood of my life ever since she appeared. "I was just thinking about how you called me a forest ranger. Then I realized I was the one who set up the volunteer schedule for the group of us who drive past the trailhead daily." Leaning down, I give her a slow, deep kiss. "Ever since you've given me my job title, I honestly feel more centered. Thank you."

"Were you always the tree hugger in your family?" she asks, grinning.

"The forest was just what I gravitated to. Jonah was destined to be a medic. Josh was born to be a woodworker. My cousins have all fallen into the roles they are perfectly suited for."

"Which is how you ended up as the guy who picks up stray girls you find lurking in the woods?"

"Guess so," I chuckle as I set fried eggs and toast in front of her, then bring over a dish of sliced fruit for us to share. As I sit down with my own eggs and toast, I slide my chair closer so that our knees can touch. "Did you sleep well, gorgeous?"

"Yes. It was amazing." She looks up at me through long, dark lashes. "I haven't been sleeping well for weeks, ever since I realized that Brad was up to no good. Then not at all after I realized that he was after me. Having you right beside me is like having my own personal bodyguard."

"Are you *sure* he's after you, though?" I hate seeing her face droop into a frown.

"He screamed at me for ages when I suggested keeping the app fair for everyone," she whispers. "I wasn't focused on the money."

Her eyes meet mine. "I should've known he was sketchy. He started ranting about his 'family's' money, and I don't think he meant blood family, if you know what I mean. I didn't even know there were people like that *in* Kingsville."

The thought of Kara having anything to do with the mafia, even second hand, makes my shoulders tighten and my fists clench. "Did he lay one single finger on you?" I watch her eyes carefully, knowing already she tends to downplay what has happened to her.

"No. Just screaming. And a lot of threatening. But that was before I locked him out of the data, so..."

I hate to ask, but I have to. "What do you think he would do if he caught up with you?"

Kara looks up at me with fearful, haunted eyes. "Get the passwords out of me any way he could? He wants that app online immediately. He's made a lot of promises to a lot of people. It sounds like I only knew a tiny fraction of what was going on behind the scenes. Money laundering, and...who knows what all else."

It breaks my heart that Kara presses her lips into such a straight line, as if she refuses to look sad. She's far too stoic for such a lovely young woman. She shouldn't have to be that strong alone.

"Baby," I murmur softly, reaching out to thread our fingers together. "I'm no security expert, but I think you did everything right."

"Except my car and phone and everything are at the bottom of the mountain. If he tracked those, it would lead him to this vague area."

"But then you could have hitched a ride south, or gotten on a plane, or—"

"He knows I don't have any money."

"Does he know your entire family history? Every single one of your friends?"

She shrugs. "It's just me and a handful of friends from college. We haven't been super close over the past few years, but yeah... I suppose I could be staying with a friend of a friend, or whatever. And he knows that I was a waitress, so I could've looked for work anywhere in the country."

"Well, there you go." I squeeze her hand, then release it so that she can dig into her eggs before they get too cold. "I've already got people in town watching for him. I doubt that he'd hike through the forest on his own. Plus, nobody here has seen you. They couldn't even respond to a description no matter how much he threatened them, right?"

Kara brightens. "You're right!"

"So your mission today, should you choose to accept it, is figuring out whether you'd like to go for a walk or a drive this afternoon, a little light relaxing, and then later maybe we'll make dinner together?"

Her lovely blue eyes glow as she stares at me, slowly nodding and biting her lip for a moment. She hesitates before saying, "A girl could get used to this mellow country life."

My heart pounds in my chest as if it's trying to escape, but I try to keep my expression calm as I smile gently.

"Shh, that's my master plan," I whisper, picking up my fork. "Don't tell anyone, though."

9

KARA

Jace and I spend a perfect day together. We take a short walk in the morning and cook a nice lunch together. Then a longer afternoon walk where we see some crows, ruffed grouse, and a cute blue-winged warbler with an odd white triangle patch on his shoulder.

Our big dinner feels like a party for two. Then we watch a cheesy action-romance movie before starting to get ready for bed. It's super domestic, and almost feels like we're together and our lives are like this all the time. An unlikely but real couple.

I know it's all just a fantasy, a strange chunk of time where I'm trapped here due to a weird situation. Being chased and stalked, then a bridge washing out and trapping us together? I mean, Jace is so kind to take me in, but let's face it, it's been an unusual chain of events.

But the thing is, *it doesn't feel random*. I feel more energized and grounded than I ever have before. My usual shy nervousness just doesn't seem to exist here in Jace's amazing house surrounded by the peaceful forest.

Partly because I know that Jace could protect me from

anything up to and including a bear. Even though he teased me for not just handing him the stuck jam jar this morning, or asking for his help when fishing a bowl down from a high shelf. What? I've never had anyone to turn to before, so it's not instinctive on my part. I've always taken care of things myself.

A thick arm snakes around my waist as we head for the bedroom. "I was thinking of a quick shower," he breathes against my ear. "Care to join me?"

My lower belly flutters. Naked and wet with him... There's only one way that ends. For a split second I wonder if I'm ready. But this kind of intimacy is something I've dreamed of, and Jace is so caring that he'd definitely be perfect for my first time.

His fingers shift to splay across my stomach, pulling my back against his chest. "Yeah," I breathe. "Good idea."

Jace turns me to face him, a gorgeous grin transforming his slightly rough face. "Let me help you, then. Yes?" He waits for me to nod before gripping the bottom of my shirt and lifting it up over my head and arms. Dropping to his knees, he lifts his head and pulls my breast into his mouth. "I love that you don't wear bras, gorgeous."

My nipple is so sensitive against his lips that I nearly cry out. Ripples of lust begin growing deep in my core, along with a large dose of curiosity. I can't wait to see what happens.

It feels like he's being cautious as he slowly pulls my pants and underwear down. Then he backs me up to the bed so that I plop down, my feet lifting so he can slip off my socks. I sit, almost shivering in anticipation as I stare up at him.

Jace smiles casually as he straightens up, peeling off his snug t-shirt to reveal a physique that belongs in an action movie. I'm so busy staring at his sculpted abs and the grooved lines above his hips that I don't notice at first when his pants and shorts drop to the floor. But when I do...

I've definitely felt his erection several times when we've snuggled, but seeing it up close and personal is frankly a bit terrifying. Since every part of Jace is large, it's no surprise that his cock is as long and thick as a tree branch. The shaft looks like it's straining, the thick blunt tip bobbing slightly in front of him.

His rough thumb caresses my cheek gently. "Shall we?"

I follow him into the bathroom. He turns the shower on, waits for a moment, then gets in, extending a hand to me. As soon as we're wet, naked, and face to face, he slips an arm around my waist. Soft music fills the snug space as he turns me in a slow circle while humming. Dancing makes it easier for me to relax a bit. I've never been naked with a man, but the rhythm of the tune allows me to shift my hips, rubbing gently against him.

Slowly we explore, under the pretense of lightly skimming cedar-scented soap over each other's bodies. Our slow, languorous movements soon turn our energy as steamy as the now-foggy mirror.

His palms move slowly around my breasts, and I sigh contentedly as I look up at him. He sets the soap aside, wets his hand, then slowly moves it between my legs. My thighs part automatically. Giving myself to this man seems second nature. As if my body knows I'm doing the right thing.

He holds me close as his thick fingers spread me open, caressing my slippery skin. The way he roams around every curve and dip is possessive, like he couldn't stop even if he wanted to. It feels like he needs me. For the first time ever, I feel important.

The blunt tip of his finger circles around my clit several

times before dipping inside me. My legs tighten and shake until I nearly slip. Jace catches me, chuckling as he pins me against the glass. Then he blinks in the hot steam, looking suddenly serious. "I've laughed more with you than I ever have with anyone else. Maybe that's a sign."

A sign of what? I want to ask, yet I can't think clearly enough to form the words. I gasp as his finger slides deeper, stroking rhythmically as his massive, muscular body presses against mine. My hand is gripping his hip, my thumb almost touching the tip of his shaft. Moving as slowly as he is, I skim my hand all the way up and down his length. I smile involuntarily when I feel the shiver that runs through him.

"You like that?" he whispers over the murmur of the falling water. "You like knowing how hot I am for you?"

"Yeah." It feels like his thick cock jumps in my hand when I say it. Carefully moving my palm over and around his length, I wash him in the hot stream of water that splashes between us.

Then I gasp, my knees almost buckling as he nudges a second finger inside me. Jace freezes. "You're really tight, Kara. Have you ever..."

"No. But I want to."

A deep shudder runs through him. "Maybe we should wait."

Stretching up, I kiss him lightly. "Jace. I *really* want to." His deep eyes are fixed on mine as I grin. "If you want me to beg, I will."

"Mmm." His body shifts, until he's stroking himself slowly against my palm in time with the rhythm of his fingers moving inside me. "I've wanted you from the first second I looked into those gorgeous eyes, Kara. Are you on the pill or anything?" His rich voice sounds rough.

"Yes."

"Good." His thumb finds my clit at the same time his mouth covers mine. The shower drowns out my moans as his thick fingers grind deeper, stretching me open. Jace's massive frame seems to grow, taking up the entire shower stall, making me feel so small and delicate beside him.

Everything becomes blurry and too intense as I clutch at him desperately, pinned between his muscles and the slightly cool glass. Jace is clearly about to make me come to get me ready to take... When we... I'm finally going to... My hand grips his shaft perhaps a little too tightly, and he groans as I spill over the edge, the climax sizzling through my veins as I gasp for air.

"So hot," he growls, his thumb swirling harder against my clit as his fingers pump fast and deep inside me. "I can feel your tight little pussy getting all nice and ready for me."

Moaning, I writhe in his arms, still coming hard as he nibbles under my ear. As my fingers skim over the tip of his shaft, I can feel a wetness there that's a little bit different from the hot water all around us.

As soon as I'm able to breathe again, Jace captures my lips. "Do you want me, baby?"

"Yes. Please."

I feel like I'm having an out of body experience as he lifts me off my feet, holding me up with one arm while shielding me from the spray with his shoulder. His right hand positions my thigh around his hip, then grasps his length. As the thick blunt head runs through my still quivering pussy, I realize this is it. The moment I've wondered about and anticipated for years.

I'm so glad that Jace is the one I'm sharing it with.

We both groan as his body enters mine just an inch. Then the side of his jaw tightens. "I'm trying so hard to be gentle, gorgeous, but you're really tight."

"Is that bad?"

He brushes his nose against mine. "Not at all. It's sexy as hell. I just don't want to hurt you. Tell me if it's too much, okay?"

"Okay." Every single thing about this encounter is "too much", but in the good way, making me want even more.

Jace slowly begins to push deeper, and I can feel the tension in his muscles. Feel his hips flex and arms tighten as he holds me safely. Feel that I'm completely under his control.

I love it, I think... Oh, *wow*. All of the air leaves my body in a whoosh as he presses even deeper and the realization creeps through my mind like the first rays of the sun lighting up the distant hills at dawn.

I think I'm falling in love with Jace. I hope it's not just some reaction to my current stress. It can't be. It feels so very real.

And as he moves deeper inside, igniting every nerve and creating a spinning tornado of sensations that tears right through me, I realize he is the only thing in this world I've ever craved like this.

10

JACE

Every touch, every caress tells me I've finally found what I've been searching for my entire life. Kara's energy is what I've been missing. Her sweet essence gives me purpose.

Not to mention, her hot little body against mine makes me feel like a savage. My cock has never been so hard as it pulses, and slipping gently inside her tight wet pussy feels unbelievable.

Kara shifts, her other leg wrapping around me as her ankles cross behind my ass. I can't stop caressing her every-where I can reach, stroking her petal-soft skin as she quivers against me. I shouldn't be taking her like this for her first time, wet and raw with me barely in control. Yet it's perfect. My sweet girl trusts me. Needs me as much as I need her.

Kara's breath catches, and her soft little hums become unsteady. I feel her snug pussy soften and open, and then I plunge in all the way to the hilt. "Yes," she moans, and I cut her off with a deep, breathy kiss.

"Is that what you need, gorgeous? You need me nice and deep inside your sweet pussy?"

"Uh huh." Her eyes are glazed over, her mouth open as she presses her full, round breasts against my chest. Her fingers clench across the back of my shoulders as she holds on for the ride of her life.

I twist, putting just enough space between us that I can slide my hand in, caressing around the top of her slick folds until I find her clit. She gasps loudly, and I feel her nails prick my skin. As I fall into a steady rhythm of deep thrusts and my thumb gently rubbing her clit, Kara begins to tremble harder.

"You're perfect," I growl. "Gorgeous and sweet and everything I've ever dreamed of and more. The only thing that could make this moment more perfect is if I felt your hot little pussy coming all over my cock."

Her lovely blue eyes fly wide open, then she nods.

"You like that, my pretty girl? When I tell you what's going to happen?"

Her chin tips up and down quickly. Pinning her tightly against the wall, I breathe into her ear. "You drive me crazy, baby. It's a good thing we're already in the shower. Because I'm going to pump you so full of my come that it would be a huge mess anywhere else."

She lets out another shaky moan, and her fingers dig even harder into my skin. My shaft is a bar of steel inside her softness, thrusting deeper, faster, until she begins to whimper while smiling. The soft heat and tight grip of her pussy around me is sexy as hell, but it's that twinkle in her eye that does me in.

Kara is so sinfully sweet in all the right ways. Most importantly, Kara is my girl.

A wave of possession rolls through me, straight down my spine. I might be becoming obsessed with her. This girl I found in the forest is everything I didn't know I needed.

Her soft noises turn into stuttering, mewling, confused gasps as I rub her clit harder. I can feel her tightening around me, every deep stroke making my thighs and balls clench. My stomach muscles are quivering from the force needed to hold myself back.

The temperature of the hot water splashing around us begins to drop, but I couldn't stop now even if it turned to ice. "Come for me, baby," I rasp, staring deeply into her eyes. "Let me feel you come."

She starts to nod, then her head snaps back against the wall as she inhales sharply. "Jace..." she mutters, just as I feel her snug body tighten all around me. "*Yes...*"

I saw that Kara was perfectly beautiful in the first second that I could make out the details of her face in the dark forest. Now, though, she's even more stunning — flushed and squirming, lush pink lips open wide as she cries out through her climax.

"My sexy, beautiful girl," I grunt, staring into her eyes as I grind faster, deeper, sending her over the edge until I feel everything release. The satisfaction of filling her with burst after burst of my wet heat is so draining that I almost wobble. Yet I manage to keep her securely pinned against the wall, holding her until we catch our breath.

Then I set Kara gently back on her feet, keeping an arm around her. She looks up at me in surprise. "Wow. You weren't kidding."

"About...?"

I think if she weren't so flushed, she would blush. "About... You know. There being a lot of it. *Huge* mess."

I burst into laughter, hugging her close. Then I aim the water between her legs so she can rinse herself clean.

We get out before the water gets too cold, and I towel her off thoroughly before she throws one of my t-shirts over her head.

I yank on some shorts, then tuck us into bed. This time she doesn't play coy, diving right into my arms. "You feel really good right here," I murmur, stroking her hair as her head nestles into the front of my shoulder.

"And you feel really good right here." Her palm spreads across the center of my chest.

Kissing her forehead gently, I give her a loving squeeze, and make sure the blankets wrap around her perfectly. She's already half asleep as I reach over to snap off the light.

Her breathing becomes softer and more regular, and I think she's out, but then I hear a whisper. "Jace?"

"Yeah, baby?"

"Thank you."

I caress her shoulder. "Pretty sure I'm the one that should be thanking you. But what for?"

She strokes my chest again. "For...well, everything. But especially for making me feel safer than I ever have before."

"That's what I'm here for, baby. To keep you safe."

Her sweet giggle echoes through the dark. "Because you're the forest ranger and you keep everyone safe."

I snort. "Sure. Let's go with that."

Kara's breathing slows again, and I stay completely still until I feel her body relax completely. It means so much that she really does trust me. I get the sense that her life has been a bit rough. I find that extremely disturbing.

Well, not anymore. My darling girl is going to be safe, protected, and stress-free. I'm not sure how, but I'm going to see to it.

Plus, I'm going to make sure that Kara is on board with being my girl.

No matter how certain I am about that, I need to hear it from her luscious lips before I will truly believe this is happening.

11

KARA

After another fantastic breakfast and lunch, where Jace and I somehow manage to chat about everything and at the same time nothing at all, I notice that I'm becoming incredibly comfortable with him. Yet every time he casually touches me, I feel electrified. Is this the beginning of twinges of love? I have no way of knowing, no frame of reference. But it feels like maybe it is.

We walk along one of his private trails deep in the forest, holding our coffee flasks. Even the silence is companionable with Jace. He's clearly not a naturally chatty person. Sometimes I feel like he's forcing himself to speak more, in order to make things comfortable for me. I appreciate the effort, but I don't want him to change himself on my account.

We reach a breathtaking, picturesque lookout point that showcases the entire valley. Clouds are gathering, and the mountaintops are far closer than I expected. Jace stops, pulls out his phone, and turns it on.

He thumbs through his texts, nodding. "The bridge is open again. Do you want to drive down and get your car? I can search it for tracking devices. You can leave your phone off and follow me up the mountain. Then we'll hide your car in my garage."

I love that he takes my paranoia so seriously. "Perfect. Thanks."

"It sounds like you left your car near Spring Grove. If that's the case, we have no choice. We have to pop into the bakery for pie."

I laugh at the way he waggles his eyebrows. "Sure."

"First we'll go into Old Hemlock Valley to fuel up the truck and get road snacks for us." He pauses, watching my eyes carefully. "What about my earlier idea of bringing my laptop and you using the library Wi-Fi to email your friends and let them know you're okay?"

I instinctively grab his hand and squeeze it. "Thank you. That's a great suggestion. Amber and Kate will be worried since I skipped our weekly video chat."

He wraps an arm around me, holding me close. "Good. Let's just breathe in the mountain air for a moment, then we can get going."

After staring out at the lush rolling hills in silence for a few more minutes, we both nod decisively at the same time, then walk back to the house.

On the drive into town, we take the bridge that had been washed out. Just a few days ago it would have been impossible for me to imagine living so far from a city. Just the thought of it would have scared me to pieces. But Jace seems prepared for any emergency. He's a true mountain man, strong and capable. Such a force of nature himself that he's totally at one with nature.

As we drive through Old Hemlock Valley, I grab a worn gray baseball cap from the seat between us, jamming it low over my eyes as I scrunch down in my seat. Jace grins, squeezing my knee. "Do whatever you need to do to feel comfortable, baby. Even though there aren't a lot of cameras around here."

"Yeah, but didn't you say that there's a small hotel?"

He glances at me sharply, then frowns. "You're right. Stay down. Although, really, would this guy come up the mountain and start searching door to door for you?"

I shrug noncommittally, looking out at the beautiful, quaint streets of the town, just like an old-fashioned, timeless village. I find myself idly wondering what it would look like all lit up and blanketed in snow at Christmas-time. And I notice that over half of the people we pass, whether on the sidewalk or in other vehicles, give Jace a nod and wave as we go by. "Everyone really does know you here."

"Yup. *One of those nice Wolfe boys.*"

There's something in his tone that makes me think he's almost embarrassed that his family is so well-known. Strange. I'll have to ask him about that someday.

Jace parks around the back of the lovely stone library, then hurries me in via the side door. The librarian gives him a bright smile, and nods when he gestures inquisitively at the corner. He sets up his laptop in a small side conference room for about six people.

"Once in a while, my internet gets knocked out during storms, and it takes a while to fix it," he explains. "Mrs. Honeywell lets me work here whenever I need to. Plus, the printer is a lot better than mine."

He launches a browser with a VPN running that makes it look like we're somewhere in Canada. I log into my email and send a quick message to a few select friends without telling them where I am, simply making a vague reference to having "gone out west for a while". I hate lying to them, but I have to be cautious.

Once that's done, I take a deep breath and skim the

subject lines of the emails Brad has sent me over the past week.

"What is it?" Jace asks, obviously seeing my pained expression.

"I don't know whether I should read Brad's emails or not." My voice sounds weak, and I hate that this stupid ex-business partner is making me feel positively sick to my stomach, even from a safe distance.

"Don't," Jace says quickly. "It's just going to make you feel like shit. If you want, I can skim through them and give you the highlights. Does that work?"

"Could you?" I spin the laptop toward him, angling the screen so I don't have to look.

"Of course." His warm, firm palm cups my cheek. "And, for the record, it means a lot to me that you would just hand me your email like this," he says gently. "I love that you trust me this much, Kara."

I grin. "It's the least I can do for you, letting me be queen of your entire kitchen."

He leans over to kiss my forehead, then angles the laptop even further away. I watch nervously as his eyes track back and forth. Jace is doing an admirable job of keeping his expression relatively neutral but there's a subtle tightening in his jaw and wrists, and a stiffness comes into his shoulders. Whatever he's reading is clearly filling him with barely contained rage.

"What an arrogant, ignorant piece of *shit*," he finally mutters through clenched teeth. "This little worm took your entire app — something that was supposed to promote artists and help the average person discover fine art that they liked — and turned it into a money laundering device for the mafia." Jace looks at me with an eyebrow cocked. "At least, that's what he's claiming. He's yammering on about his friends and a couple of cousins who are apparently well-connected, blah blah fucking blah. I wouldn't be surprised if he's just exaggerating for the sake of dramatic effect."

"Yeah, sounds about right." I hesitate. "So he's screaming that he's going to hunt me down?"

Jace nods, glowering. "Yup. He sounds like a snot-nosed little prick who's been spoiled rotten his entire life." Jace is seething. "I can't stand that he made you so many promises, baby. That he lied to you."

"It was partly my fault. I was an idiot for trusting someone I didn't know very well," I say. "I should have checked out his credentials."

Jace shakes his head. "Nah. Credentials can be faked. You don't really know someone until you look them in the eye, shake their hand, and have a coffee with them. It's *not* your fault, Kara." He snaps the laptop shut and grasps my hands. "None of this is."

I can feel my bottom lip trembling. I have no idea how scared I should be, and ironically that makes it even more terrifying. My hands are trembling, my knees are shaking. It even feels like this little meeting room is closing in on me. "Did it sound like he's coming after me?"

His gorgeous lips press into a firm line. "That's what he's threatening, yes. But he clearly doesn't have any idea where to start. I wouldn't be surprised if he asks your friends and any other connections he can find online."

"That's why I just told my friends that I headed west." I wink.

His eyes light up. "I love that my girl is a smart cookie."

His girl. My heart actually flutters.

"Hey." Jace kisses my forehead softly, then takes my hand as we leave the room. "Are you ready to go down to Spring

Grove? I have to stop and ask Mrs. Honeywell if my books are in, then we can grab a coffee next door and get going."

"Sure. Can I use the bathroom here first?"

He points to the back corner of the building. "I'll meet you at the front in a minute."

After I'm done, I meander slowly through the library, relishing the calmness that always floods me when surrounded by endless books. By the time I get to the front door, I see that a beam of sunlight is illuminating the whole front entrance. Amazing.

I step outside, staying in the entryway, enjoying the warmth on my face on what up till now has been such a cloudy day. An old man gives me a friendly nod from his spot on the bench a few feet away. Across the street, a woman laughs with her toddler as he pushes his own stroller for half a block.

There aren't a lot of vehicles parked around town in the middle of the day, but I do note three slightly dirty pickup trucks that are obviously owned by farmers, and a midsize blue SUV with car seats in the back.

There's a glint of silver down the street, then the sun disappears behind a cloud. Leaning forward, I peer around the corner and see the rest of the Mercedes.

Then I see an all too familiar figure coming out of the hardware store across the street.

Brad.

I jump back into the doorway. My heart leaps into my throat as white hot panic floods my system.

He's going to see me if I stay here. But if I go back into the library, I'll be trapped.

What can I do?

Run.

Brad is ridiculously fussy and hates getting dirty. He'd be reluctant to follow me into the woods.

Still as a statue, barely breathing, I wait until he turns in the opposite direction. Then I dart down the street, running past two buildings until I find an alley to duck into.

Racing blindly toward a forested area two blocks away, all I can do is hope I know the way back to Jace's house.

And that Brad hasn't seen me. Won't catch me. Won't ever scream at me like that again.

Or do...whatever he plans to do to get those passwords.

12

———

JACE

Mrs. Honeywell is very apologetic but explains that the books I had requested haven't come in yet. I assure her that's fine, then we end up chatting for a moment about an upcoming town meeting about how to boost local tourism in a responsible way.

Kara comes out of the bathroom, and I watch her wander through the stacks for a moment. I love that she finally looks like she's starting to relax here.

When she steps outside into the entryway, I want to stop her. I don't want her outside alone even for a split second. Yet I don't want to be rude to the sweet librarian. Plus, of course, I don't want to feed Kara's fears. There's no conceivable way anyone could harm her in the ten seconds it would take me to get to the door.

So I keep chatting to Mrs. Honeywell, then thank her, then turn back to the front entryway.

Kara is gone.

Racing to the door, I peer down the sidewalk in one direction and another. Nothing.

Something clicks when I see a silver Mercedes across the

street. My hands are already fists, blood pounding through my veins.

"Did you see the girl that was just standing here?" I ask Mr. Yates from his perpetual perch on the bench out front.

"Tiny little thing? Long dark hair? Yeah, she was just here."

"Where did she go? Was she with anyone?"

"No, she was alone." He shrugs. "Think she saw something that freaked her out. One second she's standing there with the sun on her cheeks, then she tears off in the other direction." He points. "She went down the laneway next to the shoe store."

"Thanks," I mumble, already running full tilt, my laptop bag banging on my hip as I pelt down the alley.

Straight ahead is a parking lot, a small street with storage units...and the edge of the forest. She must've made a break for it.

Shit.

I can't call her – she doesn't have her phone with her. Even if she goes somewhere else for help, there's no way for her to contact me, since she doesn't have my number. Maybe she might get lucky and run into someone I know... or, more likely, people that just know of me.

Running toward the edge of the woods, I know that she's probably way ahead of me – especially since my poor sweet baby is probably cranked on panic and raw adrenaline.

I wait until I'm a good fifty feet into the woods to cup my hands around my mouth and holler. "Kara!" Standing perfectly still, I hear nothing but a few birds and the swish of the treetops as the wind picks up.

"*Kara!*" I bellow again. "It's Jace. Come back!"

Nothing.

Peering to the west, My gut twists as I notice storm

clouds are gathering. This can't be happening. I will not allow my girl to be out here in the woods alone, wet, and cold. Not to mention scared. I'm going to have to round up some help to find her before it gets dark.

But even before that, I'm going to find the bastard who made her run in the first place.

13

KARA

After having Brad's threats echoing through my ears and mind for the past week, I feel a strange emotion come over me. It's past panic. Beyond fear. It's like my body has taken over from my brain and decided to put as much distance between us no matter what.

My heart pounds, arms, legs and lungs pumping as I make my way through the forest. There was a bit of a trail off that side street at the beginning – a little path that locals probably use for a short stroll on their lunch breaks. Once that disappeared, it became much more difficult, but my legs refuse to slow down.

Hopping over the smaller branches is relatively easy, even though I wobble on my left ankle a few times. But leaping over large logs becomes more and more challenging. I keep trying to keep my sense of direction, hoping that I didn't get mixed up during the relatively short drive from Jace's house to the library.

If I'm able to find a well-maintained path, there's a very good chance that it's Maple Trail, which I should be able to follow back to the trailhead. I'm not one hundred percent sure I can find Jace's house from there, but I have to try. At the very least I should be able to see the top of the mountain from there, and gauge direction and distance a little better.

My hands keep alternating between clenching into fists and fanning my fingers out for fear I'm going to fall on my face. Normally I'd be admiring the lush greenery all around me, but with my pulse hammering in my ears and my knees wobbling, it's all I can do to stay upright and keep my line of vision locked ten feet in front of me.

It's hard to keep track of time, but eventually I find a trail. It's not at all well maintained, but at least it's a path that goes vaguely in the direction I want. I think.

A small break in the trees shows thick, ominous clouds gathering. Even though my breath is getting labored, I fight to keep going and keep up a medium jog. My muscles are starting to ache, and eventually I'm forced to slow my pace a bit. A tiny part of my mind is desperately trying to calculate how long it would take to jog a distance that took us around fifteen minutes to drive, but that was on roads and my feet are moving through leaves and brush and I'm too tired and frazzled.

I hope Jace isn't angry with me. I *know* he's going to worry. And he's going to wonder why I didn't ask him for help.

Tears fill my eyes as I realize I made a really stupid decision. I'm just not at all used to having anyone to rely on. My instinct to take off at top speed kicked in before I remembered that I have help now. Back up. A partner.

No. It's way too early to think like that. Even though it feels right, it would be foolish to trust someone completely when I have only known them a handful of days, even though I want to believe in us, so much.

Maybe it's just my string of bad luck talking, but no... I

really feel like Jace is the one. I've never felt such electricity when someone touched me. Never had someone listen to me with such intensity.

And now I've gone and shown him that I don't really trust him. Terrific.

How will he ever forgive me when my gut instinct was to run away from him instead of asking for his help? That's not what a proper girlfriend does.

My cheeks are wet, even though the rain hasn't started quite yet, and a damp chill is settling into the breeze angling through the trees.

I need to get a sense of where I am before the rain kicks in. Through my tears, I search for a place to get a little more height. I notice a slight cliff wall with a clearing at the top, so I begin to climb. There seem to be a lot of jutting rocks for handholds, so it shouldn't be too hard—

Wait. I'm not thinking clearly. How do I know I'm doing the right thing? Although... I'd rather face a bobcat or a storm than have Brad yell at me. Or do whatever else he might do to get that information.

It was clear from the deliberate non-expression on Jace's tight face as he read those emails that Brad was threatening some extremely unpleasant things. I know for sure he's the kind of guy to follow through, too, which scares me to the bone.

What am I doing? I have no experience dealing with this sort of thing. I'm just a bookworm art lover who wants to connect people with art they love. How am I supposed to face someone like Brad?

I can't think. Just have to pick a direction, hope it's the right one, and go.

Getting to Jace's house is the only thing I should worry about right now.

Unless, of course, Brad is following me.

14

JACE

Fire flows through my veins as I race toward the silver Mercedes. The owner isn't in sight, but one well-placed shove of my boot sets off the alarm. My eyes dart around every doorway of the main street area until I see Brad's weaselly face poking out of the hardware store.

The second I start to stride purposefully toward him, his irritated expression turns wide-eyed. Rounding on his designer heel, he takes off, running full tilt away from me. I follow at a brisk jog, confident that he won't get far.

Sure enough, a large man steps out of the fruit market, causing Brad to nearly collide with him. The man's chin jerks up to see me in hot pursuit. In a flash, his shopping bag is on the ground with apples tumbling out the top and my old friend Riggs has Brad in a headlock.

As I approach, Riggs is chuckling darkly. "If a Wolfe is chasing you, you've done something wrong, buddy."

"Let me go!" Brad screeches, trying to squirm out from under the thick arm around his throat, twisting and jerking. "I don't even know him."

My hand lands heavily on Brad's shoulder as Riggs

releases his hold just enough to let the rat's head turn toward me. "Why are you after Kara?" I growl into his dark, beady eyes.

His already pale face goes even whiter. "H-how do you know her?"

Riggs shakes him roughly. "You only get to answer questions, not ask them, asshole."

To his credit, Brad seems to realize that he's completely out-gunned, and the only chance of getting out of this in one piece is to be agreeable.

"Kara was working for me. When the project was almost finished, she changed all the passwords and ran off. She's obviously going to sell the app to the highest bidder, and screw me out of some important connections."

"Funny, that's not the version I heard. The way she tells it, you lied to her and changed the project. She didn't want to be involved anymore, so she took her proprietary information and left." My fingers dig roughly into his scrawny shoulder. "Then you threatened her. And before you try to deny it, I saw all of your emails to her." Brad's eyes almost bug out of his head.

Riggs shakes him again. "You're threatening a woman, you pathetic son of a bitch?"

"This is assault," he whines. "You can't do this to me."

Riggs and I both chuckle, and I lean in closer. "Dude, it's not assault when your family owns most of the mountain. It's more like smacking a bug away. You get my drift?" Wow. I think I can actually hear his teeth chattering.

"Jace is basically the forest ranger out this way," Riggs says casually. "He has jurisdiction. He keeps everything natural, keeps everything safe..."

"Including people under my protection." My finger stabs into the center of Brad's chest. "Especially from assholes who try to terrify a young woman into giving up her business so that you can use it for illegal purposes."

"It's not exactly *illegal* as such, it's—"

He's cut off by Riggs tightening his arm. "Buddy, just stop talking. I don't even know what the hell you've done, and I don't care. Around here, we don't treat women like that. Ever."

Brad blinks harder, and I actually begin to wonder if Riggs is cutting off his air. Then he releases him slightly, and his captive sputters with relief.

I nod. "Let's get him to my truck."

The two of us march Brad to my pickup, then I grab some zip ties from the glove box. Once his hands are secured behind his back, I fashion ankle cuffs linked by two ties, so he can't shuffle more than an inch and a half at a time. Nice work, if I do say so myself.

"Sorry," Riggs says to me, checking his watch. "I have a flight, so I need to get going."

"No problem. Thanks for your help."

I clap him on the back, then Riggs gives Brad's face a dainty slap. "You behave." He nods to me, then heads for his truck.

I shove Brad onto a bench, using more zip ties to attach his hands and one ankle to the steel bars. "I'll be calling the police to officially run you out of town once I check on Kara."

"You can't leave me like this! I'll—"

One lightning-fast backhand across his cheekbone silences him. "You'll *what*? Be held by the police for who knows long while I show them evidence that you've been threatening an innocent young girl? They won't even have time to process you before my family lawyers step in."

I lean down, looming into his face. I never bring up my

family name with strangers, but just this once, it feels appropriate. "You've seen the signs all over this mountain for businesses with the name Wolfe?"

He nods miserably.

"That's my family. We've been here as long as the trees. And everyone...*everyone* who lives here is very protective of our own." I hope that I'm not speaking out of turn, but I have to say it because I desperately need it to be true. "Kara is now one of us."

A few people have gathered around, and I see James, the lone policeman in town, coming our way.

"My family's lawyers can be vicious when it's called for," I mutter in a low voice that only Brad can hear. "You will be charged with everything under the sun. They will make it very clear that you are never to come to this area again. If you leave and never return to Wolfe Mountain, you'll just lose this one business. But if you ever come within a few hundred miles of this place ever again, or harm Kara in any way, even attempt to contact her, you'll lose everything."

My growl comes from the depths of my soul. "And, asshole... I do mean *everything*."

When I draw myself up to my full height, Brad blanches and his eyes go wide.

James strolls over, coffee in hand, and claps me on the shoulder. "Is there a problem here?"

"This piece of shit has been threatening my girlfriend. Claiming to have mafia connections, and wanting to use her app for money laundering purposes. I need to go find her before the storm moves in."

"Right." James nods without a second thought. "I'll throw him in the closet until I hear from your lawyers."

"Appreciate it."

Brad's chin trembles at the mention of the closet, which

makes me chuckle inwardly as I jog to my truck. The police facilities in Old Hemlock Valley are housed in a corner of the City Hall building, and consist of just a handful of rooms. There was no budget for a proper jail, and nobody wanted to destroy the historic building, so they simply reinforced a small walk-in closet and put in a bench.

I drive past the spot where Kara ran into the forest, thinking. She's probably headed to my house, but how good would her sense of direction be without a map or compass, or even her phone?

I'm sure she's smart enough to head to Maple Trail. Once she's on one of those paths, she can find her way to the trailhead. I hope.

Looking up, my heart sinks when I see that thick clouds are gathering fast. I'm a bit of a loner, but quick to help others. I can't think of the last time I called on my friends to help me out in return, but this is definitely an "all hands on deck" situation.

The thought of Kara out alone in the woods, scared and cold, turns my blood to ice. We need to find her.

And the second I do, I need to tell her the truth.

She's mine. I'm hers. And I'm going to make sure that she's never afraid of anyone or anything ever again.

15

KARA

My fingers ache and my knees feel all scraped up against the rocky wall as I attempt to climb the mini cliff. Finally, I get to a point where I feel like I shouldn't go any higher. I'm already afraid to look straight below me.

I've made more than a few mistakes in my life, and I'm starting to think this one is pretty high on the scale. Peering left and right, there's no way of knowing where I am, or how far it is to Maple Trail, never mind Jace's house.

Only a few raindrops have hit me so far, and the trees are providing shelter, but it's starting to get dark, so if I don't find a direction fast, I'm in big trouble.

Clamping my fingers around the edge of rock, I look carefully over my shoulder, making sure not to look down. The valley in the distance looks familiar. Is that the one we saw from the lookout near Jace's house? If so, then Maple Trail is between there and where I am now. It seems incredibly far. It could take me hours to get there.

My entire body sags. *Why* didn't I just go back into the library to get Jace? Why did I have to run?

Because you panicked. Because you're a silly girl who keeps messing everything up.

The breeze picks up. I need to decide right now whether to try to climb higher, or get back down. Then I hear something. Not the wind. More like...a call? Straining to hear, the sound floats by again.

"Kara? Kara!"

I don't think it's Brad's voice. But it's definitely not Jace. I don't recognize it.

"Kara – we're friends of Jace."

Then a second, slightly different tone. "Kara – Jace sent us to find you."

It's two different voices. Brad wouldn't know about Jace, so they're definitely trustworthy. "Over here!" I holler back, trying to climb back down the cliff.

Looking down...oh god, that makes my head swim...I'm only maybe twenty-five feet up, but it feels like a mile.

"We've found her." I turn to see two burly men heading toward me, one of them on his phone. "She looks okay."

The other man comes closer. "Kara, my name's Barrett. Can you start climbing down?"

"Yeah. I think so."

The other man is obviously on the phone with Jace, explaining where we are. Barrett focuses on me. "You're okay now. Just relax. Take a deep breath, and start backing down nice and slow."

He's standing right underneath me, but there's no way he could really catch me if I fell. I attempt to calm my ragged breathing, then reach my left foot back down to the edge I used before.

"Thaaat's it," he says quietly and encouragingly. "One step at a time."

"Jace is on his way," the other man says. As I slide my eyes to him, he smiles and waves. "Hey. I'm Griffin."

"Thanks for coming to get me." My voice sounds tiny in the wind, which is starting to bounce off the rocks and trees around us.

As I slowly move down, I hear Griffin quickly calling several people to let them know that I've been found. Wow – Jace set up a full on search party for me? That makes my heart sing.

"Let's try to get you down before it rains," Barrett says, throwing a worried glance at the sky. "Don't rush, but...yeah, keep going."

I manage to climb down a few feet more before it starts to rain in earnest. "That's it," Griffin calls up. "There's a good hold for your right hand about one foot below."

Between the two of them guiding me, I manage to make it a few more feet. It's super slow going, since I'm afraid to look down. All the way up, I could see what I was doing. Now my own body is in the way as I struggle to find hand- and footholds.

What was I thinking? I'm not a rock climber. Once again, I panicked, and as a result I'm in over my head.

I get to a point where there doesn't seem to be anywhere for me to hold on. I pause, feeling around with my left foot.

"Stretch just a bit more to the left," Griffin says. "Shift your weight slowly. You've got this, Kara."

I can just feel the piece of rock with the tip of my toe, but would have to shift too much of my weight over there at once, and I don't quite trust it since I can't see it.

"It's okay, baby. I'm right here." Looking down into Jace's deep green eyes, my racing heart calms down a bit. "You're not going to fall," he says matter-of-factly. "But on the off chance you did, there are three of us here to catch you. It's all good."

With a deep breath, I swing to the left, finding the foothold. That gives me enough leverage to scramble down several more feet.

"Just a little more, baby. Then you'll be in my arms."

I make it down a bit further before the rain really kicks in. Whatever kind of rock this is, there's enough dirt on it that the sudden deluge of water makes everything slippery. "I'm going to fall!" I yelp, trying to descend quickly without losing my grip.

"No, you're not. Just reach out to the right, down six inches."

I try to do as instructed, but my fingers slip, making my body swing out at a strange angle. I can see that I'm only eight feet above the ground now, but I'm not sure how I'd jump or land. I can't get my feet under myself from here.

Jace doesn't give me time to ponder any longer. He leaps up, his powerful legs sending him toward me as he grabs me, pulling me away from the rock and allowing us to land safely on flat ground.

He pulls my body tightly against his as I burrow my face into his chest. "I'm sorry," I sniffle. "I should've gone back inside the library. I panicked."

"Shh, it's okay, baby." He strokes my hair with one hand, then stops suddenly, simply holding me with his right arm around my hips. "You're just used to doing everything on your own. But that's over now. Okay?"

"Jace, uh, I don't mean to alarm you, but your hand is bleeding." Barrett sounds serious, making my head jerk up.

"Yeah, I can feel it," Jace grumbles. He sets me down, then looks at the back of his left hand. He must have scraped his knuckles and wrist on the rock as he pulled me away.

"I'm so sorry!" I almost start to cry, but Jace interrupts me with a swift, deep kiss.

"This is not your fault," he insists. "It's just a scratch, anyway."

Griffin steps in, grabbing Jace's arm as he takes a good look. "Dude, it's more than a scratch. Why don't you drive down and get Jonah to patch that up?"

Jace scoffs. "I have at least half the medical training he does."

"Yeah, but it's hard to work on yourself. Just do as I say, will you?" Griffin puts on a stern expression, giving me the impression these guys must be very old friends. "Barrett and I can take Kara to your house."

Jace grumbles, but doesn't argue. By the time we trudge through the darkening forest and get back to the trucks, his hand is dripping blood.

Griffin grabs some paper towel from his glove compartment and wraps it up. "Should I drive you there?"

Jace rolls his eyes. "No. Thanks, though." He pulls me against him, giving me such a fierce, deep kiss in front of his friends that I'm almost embarrassed. He isn't. It feels like he wants them to see he's claiming me. "See you at my place in half an hour, gorgeous."

I hate watching him drive away, but I do want to make sure that he's all right.

Barrett offers me a hand politely to help me up into Griffin's truck. As we start to drive, Griffin says, "We'll swing by and get Barrett's truck at the top of Maple Trail."

"Cool. Thanks."

I'm struck by the way that these guys just automatically

jump in to help their friend and me. "I really appreciate your help."

They both turn to smile at me. "Jace Wolfe is one of the finest men we know," Barrett says seriously. "We're just glad he's found a nice girl."

I give them a saucy grin. "You don't even know me. How do you know I'm nice?"

He shrugs. "Sometimes you can just tell. I knew the split second I met my girl."

Griffin chuckles. "If you have any nice friends, feel free to set me up."

Barrett snorts. "Do dirty boys deserve nice girls?"

I turn to him, raising an eyebrow. "Rude!"

"Just a fact, ma'am." It must be some sort of in-joke that I'm not getting.

Griffin rounds a corner, using the momentum to lean toward my ear. "My last name is Dirty."

"Seriously?"

"Yup. But trust me, there's no man on this mountain who wouldn't clean up for a nice girl."

We drop Barrett at his truck, then continue on to Jace's house. Barrett has a key, so we go in and I make us all coffee.

My mind races. Has Jace been up here on his mountain, hoping to find a woman? The insecure part of me wonders if he simply jumped at the first girl who wandered into his path. But I don't think so. It feels like we truly belong together. I just have to learn to trust him completely, and let go of my fears.

Because I want to be his girl. I want this crazy detour through the forest to end with the two of us together. Permanently.

16

———

JACE

My brother Jonah laughs at me at first for coming to his house with such slight scrapes. Then he takes a proper look, and sees they're much deeper than they first look. "Okay, fair, I guess you can't clean and tape these one-handed."

"Exactly. Thanks."

He doesn't even warn me before he douses my hand with stinging disinfectant. "How the hell did this happen?" he mutters gruffly as he patches me up. "Rescuing someone again?"

When I hesitate, he gives me a sharp look. He's always been able to see right through me. "Oh. Not just someone, I take it."

"Her name is Kara."

Jonah shakes his head as he wraps my cuts with pressure bandages. "Jeez, I can tell you're ass over applecart by the way you say her name."

I snort at his sad attempt at humor. "Ass over applecart? How old are you, eighty?"

"Shut it." Next he covers everything with waterproof bandages. "Keep this dry for forty-eight hours."

"Will do. Thanks."

He nods with a crooked grin. "Good luck with your girl. Glad you found someone."

"Thanks." For a split second, I see a flash of sadness in his eyes. I know Jonah has been wanting to find a good woman for a long time.

The thing is, Old Hemlock Valley is great, but it has far more men than women, since the terrain up here is so rough. I don't like thinking about my brothers and cousins living out their entire lives alone. It's depressing. I really do feel like I've won the lottery by finding Kara.

As I drive home, I start to think about the decision I have to make, even though in truth I've already decided. I need to formally ask Kara to stay with me. To live here with me on my mountain, in my town, so that I can keep her safe forever.

She obviously has a tough time trusting men, and I can't blame her. But I need her to trust me. She has to know by now that all I want is to make her happy.

Barrett and Griffin must hear my truck coming up the driveway, because they meet me on the porch. I get out of the truck awkwardly, trying not to rip the bandage open. The rain is still pelting down hard, and I rush to duck under the awning.

"Your girl makes better coffee than you do," Griffin chuckles. "All patched up?"

"Yeah, I'm good. Thanks so much for taking care of her."

I shake both of their hands, and Barrett nods. "Anytime you need us, Jace, just holler. You know that."

Kara comes to the door to wave as they call out their goodbyes. As they get into their trucks, Griffin flashes Kara a wink. "Don't forget – set me up with a nice friend who doesn't mind if her man is a little dirty. We need more women up on this mountain."

I scoop my girl into my arms, pulling her inside. "I'm sorry," she starts, but I instantly cut her off with a slow kiss. From the way her body melts into mine, I can tell that she doesn't blame me for what happened. Still, I need to say it. If I'm going to keep this incredible woman in my life, I need to start expressing myself a lot more.

"Baby, I have only been utterly terrified twice in my life: when I was four, and a huge coyote walked right through our backyard, grabbed my stuffed owl, and took off with it. And today, when I thought you might be out in the forest, hurt and alone."

Kara frowns. "And in the end, you're the one that got hurt."

I wave my hand dismissively. "It's nothing, other than an excuse for a little teasing from my brother."

She smiles sweetly. "I can't believe you called in all those people to help. No one's ever done anything like that for me before."

"I'm just sorry I didn't protect you better," I murmur, kissing across her forehead. "I should've kept you right beside me. Kept you safe so you had no reason to panic. I can't stand the thought of you out there in the woods alone."

"It's all my fault." Her head shakes against me. "I've been so high strung for the past little while that I just freaked out and ran. But I'm sorry... I should have run to you."

She relaxes more as I chuckle, keeping my arms around her. "It sounds like we both need to reprogram some old thought patterns."

"No kidding." Her chin sets with determination as her lovely eyes meet mine. "For example, from now on I'm only going to take jobs with quality people, and thoroughly check their references."

My palm slips down to circle her lower back. "Baby, what if you didn't need a job at all? I have plenty of money. Plenty of space. What if you came and lived with me?" I love the way her eyes light up. "You could get a new programmer and work on your app, or do anything else you wanted. But you wouldn't have to worry about bills."

"I've never cared about money beyond having enough to survive," she says softly. "And I'd love to live here with you." Her eyelashes flutter as she looks up at me. "I just can't believe you're asking so quickly."

Giving her a big squeeze, Kara laughs when I hold her too tightly, squishing her a bit. "Yeah, it's too fast. Who cares? I know it's right. Don't you?"

Her chin tips up and down. "Absolutely."

Then her face falls, her bottom lip trembling. "But what are we going to do about Brad?"

I grin. "Oh, he's taken care of. He's probably still handcuffed in the...well, it's the closest thing to a jail cell we have in town. He'll be dealing with my family's lawyers for a good long time, especially once we forward them all those threatening emails he sent you. And when they let him out, I guarantee he won't bother you again." I can't stifle my smirk. "I put the fear of God into him. I honestly think he may have pissed himself a little when Riggs was holding him by the throat, and I was growling in his face."

Her mouth falls open. "What?"

"Don't worry about it, baby. It's over. It'll all be dealt with over the next few days."

She squeezes her hands around my waist and back. "Thank you, Jace. Thank you so, so much."

My head dips for another quick kiss. "Anything for my girl." I glance at her quizzically. "You *are* my girl, right?"

Her smile is pure joy. "Yes. If you'd like me to be."

Her breathtaking blue eyes meet mine as I finally utter the words I've been holding back for so long. "Of course I would. I love you, Kara."

It takes her a second to find her breath. Then she whispers, "I love you, too."

It feels like my cheeks are going to split, my smile is so wide. "Good. Done." I step back and nod firmly. "Now, I don't like that you were outside for so long in just that little sweater. Would you like to take a shower? It'll warm you right up."

"Yeah. Except you can't get your hand wet."

"Says who?"

That luscious bottom lip puffs out as her hands land high on her hips. "The Queen of Showers."

"Showers too? Wow. Okay, sure."

We go into the bedroom, and I'm impressed by the way she strips her clothes off quickly this time, with only a touch of shyness when she glances back to catch my hungry stare. I follow right behind her as she adjusts the water in the shower, and gets in first. Draping my bandaged hand over the curtain rod, I manage to keep it dry while scrubbing her perfect breasts one-handed.

Kara cuddles against me in the warm spray. "You really want me to live here with you?"

"Yes. Immediately, if that works for you."

She looks up at me with a hopeful smile. "If you don't mind driving me to my car tomorrow, I can drive to Kingsville and get my things. It won't take long to clear out my apartment. Most of my furniture is crappy old student stuff. I'll just give it away."

"Do you actually think I'm going to let you out of my sight, missy?" My arm squeezes her hard enough to make her laugh. "I'll borrow a van from Griffin or Walker and go with you. We can even stay in a hotel for a few days if we have to."

"Then who will watch the forest?"

"Don't worry. I'll let some of the other guys fill in for me."

My hand begins running up and down her spine lazily, caressing her silky, soft skin. Then my palm dips lower to grab her ass lightly. "You had quite a scare today, baby. Should I put you to bed?" She smirks, looking down at the massive erection sticking up between us. "Don't worry, I can tell him to calm down if you like."

She flicks her damp hair. "No... I think I want to get closer to my protective ranger."

She grabs my cock with both hands, slowly gliding her wet fingers from the root to the tip. My groan makes her eyes grow wide. It's clear that she's still a bit shy, but working really hard on getting over it. I know the more time we spend together, the more she'll relax around me.

"You can do anything you like with your new toy," I mutter, barely holding back another groan. "But I need to taste you, baby."

"*Need* to?" Her eyebrow arches as she strokes me again, more firmly this time.

"Yeah. I was so worried it nearly made me sick. So now I need a mouthful of your hot little pussy to make it all better."

Kara's sharp inhalation tells me she approves of that idea, and she seems to forget all about my bandaged hand as I spin her away from me to face the tiled wall.

The water drums straight into her back, keeping her nice and warm as I drop to my knees. I hear her gasp as I spread her wide and drag my tongue straight across her pussy. Fortunately, with my bandaged hand clasping her stomach, it's somewhat sheltered from the spray as I tease her with my tongue, lips, and fingertips.

Feeling her body respond to mine almost makes me high. Makes me feel powerful. I can't believe I'm the one who has the honor of giving her this much pleasure.

I alternate between swiping my tongue and my fingertips through her juicy slit, then slowly work my fingers deep. It's too difficult to reach her clit with my tongue this way, so once she's twitching and breathless, I switch position. She moans desperately as I push my tongue inside her, massaging her clit and rolling it between my fingers.

Her thighs tremble as her entire body tightens. Even though the water is splashing into my eyes and my knees are uncomfortable on the tile floor, I would maintain this position for years if she asked me to. But it doesn't take long before she begins to twitch hard, crying out as her palm smacks against the glass over and over. "Yes," she chokes. "Jace... I..." Another wordless, breathy squeal as the orgasm rocks her, then her body sags.

I hold her up, gradually standing so that I can turn her as she wraps her arms around my shoulders. "How do you even do that?" she laughs weakly. "That was so intense."

"I've been waiting for you my entire life." My voice is serious. "I'd honestly given up, and then I found you. I'm going to give you everything you need, baby."

Her left hand drops, feeling between us to find my hard cock. She strokes me gently, looking up to watch the way my eyes crinkle as I smile. "I've noticed you're pretty gruff with the guys," she says. "I like that you're softer with me."

"That's so I can match you. You're soft all over." I kiss

along her shoulder. "Are you ready for round two, gorgeous?"

My left hand caresses up her back, and she instantly flinches. "Your bandages! I forgot." She reaches over to turn off the water. "We're plenty warm. Let's get you into a nice dry bed."

"But—"

Her finger lands across the center of my lips. "Shower Queen, remember?"

Before I can protest any more, Kara wraps me up in a bath sheet, drying me quickly. Then she hustles me toward the bedroom before grabbing her own towel.

My heart might explode from realizing that Kara is already comfortable enough to boss me around when need be. We're already finding our balance.

I grin darkly as thoughts of what I'm about to do to her flood my mind. This time I won't have to balance while standing up in the shower. This time I'll be able to possess my sweet girl by capturing her under me, and claim her completely.

17

KARA

It's hard to know which is making my head spin and belly flutter more – the fact that Jace has said he loves me, or knowing what we're about to do.

Our first time together in that hot steamy shower was pure lust, fueled by adrenaline and fire. As we drop our towels and slip under the sheets together, I can already tell that this is going to be so much more.

Jace slides his huge muscular frame right in beside me, his hand grazing up and down my body as he stares at me. Then he meets my eyes and smiles. "You're going to hear people talking in town about me being a grouch. A quiet loner. The guy who bitches about unprepared people out on the trails."

I giggle. "I was at least somewhat prepared, right?"

He pokes my nose. "*You* were about to camp illegally, missy. Let's not get into that." He looks at me very seriously. "I'm...lighter...with you. I like the version of myself that comes out when you're around."

"That's the sweetest thing anyone's ever said to me," I whisper.

His lips brush tenderly against mine. "I love you. And our first time was hot, but now... It's going to be hot and mean even more, yeah?"

My fingers reach around his shoulder to grab the back of his neck, pulling his mouth to mine as I nod. His palm meanders around my hip, then slides down my inner thigh, pushing my legs apart. I reach down to stroke him, his cock a hot bar of lead in my hand.

"I can't believe this thing actually fits inside me," I moan as he stretches out over me.

His deep eyes are soft as he nods. "All of the heat and humidity of the shower probably helped you stretch. I never want to hurt you, baby."

My inhalation is sharp and quick as the tip of his shaft glides up and down through my inner folds. He's so achingly gentle, even though I can't miss the tension in the tops of his shoulders. His left hand scoops under me, cradling my body as he notches his cock at my entrance. Instead of pressing in, he simply stays there, teasing me, twitching as I stare up at him.

"Do you like it when I tease you like this?" he murmurs.

"No, as a matter of fact. Get in there." Using my knee, I try to shove his butt to move him closer.

Jace chuckles. "I secretly love it when you boss me around."

Fisting the back of his hair, I stare deeply into his eyes. "At the moment, I'm the queen of this bedroom. So... Take me."

That mischievous grin lights up his eyes. "As you wish, your majesty."

His hips tilt, entering me so slowly that it still feels like a tease. I'm still warm and wet from the shower, so even though he presses deep, it's not too difficult to stretch open for him. He kisses across my cheekbone and my forehead as he finally thrusts all the way in. The feeling of being filled by the man I love makes my heart expand.

"So gorgeous," he whispers, shifting gently to pull back before sinking in again, letting me feel every single thick inch of him.

I will never get tired of admiring Jace's incredible body. My eyes wander over his torso as each sculpted part of him shifts and moves over me. My legs wrap around his hips, crossing my ankles so that I can pull him closer as I grind against him.

He changes the angle so that he's careful to brush against my clit with every stroke. All of my breath disappears, and I'm left blinking, shaking, as every single thrust brings me closer and closer to the edge.

"So fucking sexy," he growls against my ear. "Can't believe I found the girl of my dreams right there in the forest."

My entire body begins to seize up. I feel both fragile and strong as I tighten around him, the force of his thrusts increasing. Time seems to stop as our brains zone out and our bodies take over.

"I love that you were waiting for me, Kara. Love that I'm the only cock you're ever going to have."

I nod eagerly, trying not to pull his hair as I clutch the back of his neck with one hand and his shoulder with the other. Every long, deep stroke brings us closer.

"I can feel your hot little pussy tightening around me," he growls, his voice ragged. "Feel how much you need me. Feel how hard you're going to come for me."

Something about the thought of coming for him instead

of with him, feels...possessive? Obsessed? I'm not sure, but either way, it's so freaking hot. "More," I manage to whisper. "Jace... I'm so close..."

"I know. I can feel it. Feel this tight little pussy quivering all around me. God, I love the way you squeeze my cock, baby."

I'm too breathless to respond with words, so instead I just tighten my pussy around him, squeezing him even harder. Somehow, it pulls my energy inward, triggering my climax. A weak, thready scream escapes my lips as I stare wild-eyed up at him.

Jace's eyes are half-lidded with lust as his jaw tightens, shoulders clenching, hips flexing as he plunges deeper and harder. "That's it, baby..."

The sensation of his liquid heat flooding my twitching pussy flings me right into a second orgasm. "Yeah, give it to me," he growls darkly, still thrusting deep as I listen to my own rasping cries.

After a few moments of stillness, he flops down beside me, clutching me to him. We're both sweaty, breathless and flushed. As our heartbeats slowly return to normal, our fingers entwine.

He chuckles. "I can't believe you're mine. I'm the luckiest man on the mountain."

Lifting his hand, I kiss his knuckles. "And I'm completely free, thanks to you."

"We're going to be free together, baby." His eyebrow arches. "Except of course, for my forest duties."

"Maybe you'll teach me how to help?"

"Sure, if you like. When the weather is nice. We'll go hiking, and I'll teach you everything."

"I'd like that."

Snuggling into his chest, I feel like I'm home. Not only do I belong with Jace, I truly feel like I belong up here on the mountain, in the forest.

And, of course, now I'm the queen of the kitchen, the shower, and the bedroom.

EPILOGUE
JACE

** Three Years Later **

It's hard for a big guy like me to walk quietly, but after years of tiptoeing through the forest, I feel like I've been training for this moment my entire life.

I set the bottle of apple juice silently on the nightstand, then pull out the other two items I picked up at the hospital gift shop: a stuffed forest ranger bear for the lady, and a fluffy stuffed owl toy for the young gentleman.

I set them at the end of the bed, looking down at my two angels. Kara is sound asleep, clearly exhausted but with a smile on her face, her hand flopped over the edge of the bassinet beside her. Our four-hour-old son Michael is also asleep, but he's a bit twitchy, as if he's still getting used to being here in the outside world.

Placing my palm gently on his cheek, I watch as he settles, his breathing becoming as regular as Kara's. After a few moments, I walk around to the other side of the bed, carefully pulling the chair close so that I can hold Kara's other hand as she sleeps.

"The perfect family portrait."

My head jerks toward the low, soft voice in the doorway. "Hey, Jonah."

He smiles at me. "I've already spoken to her doctor. They're both doing great." He looks me up and down. "You, on the other hand, look like garbage. You need sleep."

"He's just been born. How can I sleep at a time like this?"

"Yeah, but I bet you haven't been sleeping for a few weeks, have you?"

"Of course not. I've been getting the house ready for the baby."

He shakes his head. "I'll hold you down and have a nurse give you a sedative if you don't at least close your eyes for ten minutes." I make a face, then fold my arm under my head so that I'm leaning on the edge of Kara's bed. He shrugs, then slips back out, muttering, "Good enough."

Staring close up at Kara's elegant hand, I love the way her engagement and wedding rings sparkle together in the dim light. Love the way our lives have been like a dream from the very beginning, even though I've been nervous for the past few weeks, running myself ragged as I've tried to get everything perfect so that Kara won't be stressed when we bring Michael home tomorrow.

After listening to my lovely wife and son breathing calmly for a few minutes, the exhaustion begins to settle in now that the adrenaline has worn off, and I can finally relax enough to close my eyes for just...

Want more? For a spicy extra scene (not part of the story, just a little bonus) please join the email list at
haleytravisromance.com!

Stay tuned for plenty of
hot, burly men on Wolfe Mountain!
You'll see Jonah again in **_Saved by the Surly Medic_**, coming in
August 2024.
You'll see Barrett again in **_Rescued by the Surly Woodsman_**.
You'll see Riggs again in **_Possessed by the Surly Pilot_**.
You'll see Barrett's younger brother Baz in the **_Wolfe_**
Mountain Chalet series.
You'll see Griffin again in the **_Dirty Brothers_** series starting
late August 2024.

PREVIEW
SHOCK TO THE HEART

With my smallest toolbox in hand, I knock at the front door. It flies open, leaving me staring at a willowy young woman with long, rich brown hair. Her eyes are dark blue, almost navy. She's barefoot, wearing black yoga pants with gray swirls on them, and a slouchy oversized gray sweatshirt that hangs off one shoulder.

She's also holding a small ice cube to her lip, drawing my eye to her beautiful, dark pink pout. It's the sexiest thing I've ever seen, and a charge of raw lust instantly zips up my spine.

"You can't be Ray." She removes the ice cube to smile.

"No. I'm his son, Trey."

She holds out her hand. "Electra." I nod, ignoring the fact that it's exactly the sort of name pretentious rock stars would pick for their kid. Her hand is soft and delicate, yet her grip is firm. "Thank you," she says. "I'm sorry that this is such a rush."

"No problem." Suddenly I need this to be a big job that will keep me here with her for at least a few hours. "What's with the ice cube? Some new beauty treatment?"

Electra laughs. "Yeah. I wanted that bee-stung lip look, so I intentionally shocked myself with a mic."

I laugh with her while shaking my head. "Are you okay?"

"I think so. I mean, it's just irritated, not really burned...right?"

She tips her lips up for me to get a good look. As an electrician, I guess I'm supposed to be an authority on shocks, but nothing can explain the searing hot current flowing through my veins and into my heart as I gently cup her chin to tilt her lips to the light.

I can barely stop myself from leaning forward just a few inches. To kiss those lips would be...life altering.

"You're right. No burn. The ice is a good idea, but that's probably enough for now. You don't want to irritate it even more."

"Good point." She presses the ice to her lip for just a few more seconds, then tosses it into the driveway. "Come on in, I'll show you the mean ol' outlet that attacked me."

We walk into the foyer, which is crammed full of massive photos of CC and Ryl with all manner of award-winning musicians and actors. A quick peek into the next room confirms that this place was designed to make an impression, not be comfortable.

I follow Electra down the hall, ignoring the bohemian decor to focus on the sensual sway of her hips. This girl is bewitching. Mesmerizing. Everything I've ever wanted in a woman, from her sass to her bright eyes to her ability to laugh at herself.

She's electrifying.

Shock to the Heart will be released on July 15th, 2024, and is available for pre-order now.

ALSO BY HALEY TRAVIS

Book links at haleytravisromance.com

Thin Ice - Winter Heat at Wolfe Mountain Chalet

He's a total stranger. Until I slip and fall into his arms, and then into his bed.

He claims he's a loner, but that doesn't explain why he's obsessed with me. Yet from the second he growls, "You're mine," into my ear, I want it to be true.

The Lumberjack's Quirky Girl

I probably shouldn't have ogled Braden Oakley's big axe. *Oops.*

Tall as a redwood and built like a moose, the devastatingly gorgeous lumberjack should have nothing in common with little miss artsy-pants—aka, *me.* So how come the harder I try to stay away, the more I end up wrapped up in his muscled arms begging for more of his hard...wood?

Meet all four HOT Oakley brothers HERE.

Possessing My Lily

From the second her delicate body thumped into my chest, I knew Lily was mine.

Every detail of my gorgeous, sweet girl is precious. Yet she's sensitive, and doesn't trust that we're already together. I'll find a way to prove I'm worth getting through her fears. That my possession will be the best thing for both of us.

Her New Bodyguard: Jackson

It was supposed to be a simple personal security job. But Ashley was so sexy and innocent that my need to care for her was far more than professional.

Mackton Mechanics

Rev your engines and get ready to fall for these hot mechanics! These huge, rough men are comfortable working with steel. What will happen when they're tinkering with a sweet girl's heart instead of a motor?

Fake Summer Wife

I'd always been too timid. But when a gorgeous man needed a favor and asked me out in front of the whole diner, I had to say yes... I would be his phony wife for one night.

For new release updates from Amazon, go to the author's page, then click **+Follow** near the top left.

Please join the mailing list at haleytravisromance.com for new releases, updates, discounts & freebies!